NW

D0211271

LYING
WONDERS

ALSO BY SUSAN ROGERS COOPER

The Milt Kovak Series

The Man in the Green Chevrolet
Houston in the Rearview Mirror
Other People's Houses
Chasing Away the Devil
One, Two, What Did Daddy Do?
Dead Moon Rising
Doctors and Lawyers and Such

Other Mysteries

Funny as a Dead Comic
Funny as a Dead Relative

LYING
WONDERS

Susan Rogers Cooper

Thomas Dunne Books / St. Martin's Minotaur
New York

THOMAS DUNNE BOOKS.
An imprint of St. Martin's Press.

www.minotaurbooks.com

Library of Congress Cataloging-in-Publication Data

Cooper, Susan Rogers.
    Lying wonders : a Sheriff Milt Kovak mystery / Susan Rogers
Cooper.
        p.   cm.
    ISBN 0-312-29056-X
    1. Kovak, Milton (Fictitious character)—Fiction.   2. Sheriffs—
Fiction.   3. Oklahoma—Fiction.   4. Sects—Fiction.   I. Title.

PS3553.O6235 L95 2003
813'.54—dc21

                                                    2002031893

First Edition: January 2003

10   9   8   7   6   5   4   3   2   1

To the Wallace clan—
Steve, Debbie, Mason,
Lindsay, Jeff, Justin,
Ashley, and Alexia—
for all the love,
support,
and
inspiration

ACKNOWLEDGMENTS

First and foremost, I would like to thank Vicky Gould, Anna Lujan, Lesa Craig, Laura Taylor Whatley, and the late Gary Snyder for all their support and affection over the last twelve years.

As always, and forever, I wish to thank Vicky Bijur, agent extraordinaire. And a very special thank-you to the best editor in the world, Ruth Cavin.

And then shall that Wicked be revealed, whom
the Lord shall consume with the spirit
of his mouth, and shall destroy with the
brightness of his coming:
Even him, whose coming is after the working
of Satan with all power and signs
and lying wonders,
And with all deceivableness of
unrighteousness in them that perish;
because they received not the love of the truth,
that they might be saved.

—2 THESS. 2:8–10

LYING
WONDERS

Prologue

Trent stuck his head through the opening to the women's tent. The space was empty, except for Amanda sitting on a cot.

"Manda!" he whispered. Her back was to him and she didn't move.

He walked up to her and touched her on the shoulder. Her head turned slowly toward him, a beatific smile on her face. "Trent," she said, the word taking too long to come out of her mouth. Her eyes were glassy and bloodshot, her movements stiff.

He knew a little about that. He wasn't exactly feeling like himself either. Three days of no sleep, with nothing to eat but oatmeal, rice, a few vegetables could get to you. And the singing. Oh, God, the singing. He was afraid he'd have the words and tune of "Kumbayah" running through his head for the rest of his life.

At first it had been okay. Fun, even. They were all so friendly, so welcoming. Always someone with them. Always smiling. Those beatific smiles. Couldn't even go to the damn john by himself. One of the guys always walking with him. "Let me show you the facilities," he said, smiling. Not a minute alone. Not a minute to think.

Three days and Trent was about out of his mind. And now he knew something was wrong, very wrong.

"Amanda, baby," he said, taking her arm, "let's go. Honey, we gotta go."

"Trent," she said, the smile never leaving her face. "He's coming."

"I know, baby, but we have to leave."

"He wants me here," she said, not really resisting, but not coming with him either.

He pulled her to her feet. "We have to leave, Amanda," he said sternly.

She followed him meekly, but slowly. Too slowly. It had taken a lot of maneuvering for Trent to get away from the guys who were always with him, and he didn't know how much time they had. Not much, he was sure. But he had to get Amanda out of there.

There'd been talk of a wedding. And Trent was pretty damned sure Amanda was supposed to be the bride—whether she wanted to be or not.

1

I lay as still as possible, not wanting him to know I was conscious. I could feel the slight indention on the bed as he moved toward me. I steeled myself for the inevitable. Finally, I felt the finger on my eyelid, pulling it open.

"Da?" he said. "You 'wake?"

I grabbed him, tossed him to the bed and began to righteously tummy-gum him to smithereens.

From the kitchen, Jean called, "He just ate, Milt. You keep that up he's going to vomit on the bed!"

Johnny Mac, as I call him, was laughing fit to beat the band. For such a little one, he had a deep, husky laugh. And it consumed him. If he was laughing, nothing else existed on this earth. All the books say two-year-olds are pretty much self-absorbed little creatures, and Johnny Mac was no exception to that rule. When he wanted something, he wanted it right that second, whether it was a cookie or some sugar (the kissing kind, that is).

I stopped the tummy-gumming and pulled him under the covers with me, trying to ignore the "More, Da, more."

"Settle down, Peach," I said. "Mama's gonna get p.o.'d if you go yucky on the bed."

Now there's a lot to be said for fatherhood, but I gotta admit I never saw myself in my whole near sixty years saying something about going yucky on the bed, or those other parents-of-a-two-year-old lines, like, "Don't eat the cat's tail," "Don't put those raisins up your nose," and "I told you once I told you a thousand times: Don't play with your winky in front of Aunt Jewel."

But somehow, when you've got a two-year-old, saying those things becomes second nature, and you don't even really see the strangeness of them until you stop to think about it.

Johnny Mac yawned and laid his head down on my shoulder, his little hand creeping up to stroke what remained of my hair.

"You sleepy, Peach?" I asked.

"No," he said, a thumb heading for his mouth, his favorite sleep aid.

We lay there for a while, the two of us, smelling my breakfast in the kitchen being fried up, and talking a little, as we do. Johnny Mac was into complete sentences now, but sometimes they didn't make a lot of sense to anybody but me and Jean.

The phone rang and Jean picked it up in the kitchen. My wife's been on crutches since she was a kid and contracted polio, but it's amazing how fast she can get around. After a quick second or two, she said, "Milt, it's for you."

It was Saturday morning and one thing I sure as thunder didn't want to do on a Saturday morning was take any calls from the office. I'm sheriff of Prophesy County, Oklahoma, and a call on a Saturday morning more than likely means something bad's happened that I'm going to have to take care of.

4

I pulled my pants off the trunk at the foot of the bed and slipped them on; never been big on talking on the telephone in my underwear.

When I picked up the phone, Jean hung up the extension in the kitchen.

"Kovak," I said.

"Milt?"

"Yeah?" I said, wondering who it was. It was a woman's voice, but it wasn't Gladys our clerk down at the sheriff's department, because she didn't work Saturdays, and it wasn't Jasmine Bodine, my one and only female deputy, because Jasmine's Eyeore voice I would have recognized in a heartbeat. For one thing, the "Milt" would have been about five syllables long. "Who's this?" I asked.

"Milt, it's Laura."

I sat there on the side of the bed for I don't know how long, my hand clinching the receiver like I could choke the life out of it.

"Yeah?" I said, carefully.

"Milt, I really need your help."

"How's that?"

"Trent's gone. I think he's been kidnapped."

Trent was Laura's oldest son, and I had to do some calculating to figure how old he'd be by now. Well into his teens.

"Teenagers do that," I said.

"I think he's been kidnapped," she said again.

"Uh-huh," I said.

And that's when she began to cry.

I hung up the phone and walked into the kitchen. Johnny Mac was on the floor in the breakfast room, running toy trucks back and forth. Jean was just serving up my eggs, sunny-side up the way I like them.

"Who was that?" she asked.

I took a breath and let it out. "Laura," I said.

Jean just gave me a look and went on with the breakfast, using one crutch to make her way to the table.

In the almost three years Jean and I had been together, I'd told her a thing or two about Laura Johnson. Some of this and some of that. But I never did tell her that for a while there, Laura Johnson had been the air I breathed, the water I drank, the food I ate. I never did tell her there were times when I thought I might die if I didn't hear her voice, or see her face, or smell her scent. That touching her hand had been like two hours of foreplay with a mortal woman.

But women are funny creatures. They've got senses men just don't have. And one of those senses is the one that tells them when another woman is or was something really special. There was no doubt in my mind that Jean knew exactly what had gone on between Laura and me, and knew exactly how much I'd hurt.

Laura and I hadn't lasted long, and when it ended it had ended just about as bad as something like that could possibly end, and Jean knew about that for sure because I'd told her.

Jean set her own plate down at the breakfast table—juice, coffee, unbuttered wheat toast, and a slice of melon—while I sat down in front of my once-a-month allotment of bacon, grits, fried eggs and buttered toast.

She didn't look at me.

"What did she want?" Jean finally asked, still not looking at me.

"Got some trouble with her oldest boy," I said, my eyes on my eggs.

"Hum," Jean said.

"Um," I said.

Johnny Mac crawled under the breakfast table and began

playing with my feet and giggling. "Gonna get you," I said, but he and I both knew my heart wasn't in the play.

"John, out from under the table," Jean said.

He scooted out and crawled into her lap, his hand heading for the jelly on the table.

"What's the problem?" Jean asked.

"Huh?" I said, like the subject had escaped my mind.

"With Laura's oldest?"

"Oh. Probably run away. She thinks he's been kidnapped."

"What makes her think that?" Jean asked, like we discussed Laura Johnson and her thought process every day of the damned week.

I shrugged. "This and that," I said.

Jean didn't say anything and I realized a little late that I shouldn't have said that. Too noncommittal, like I was keeping something from her. So I said, "Something about hanging out with the usual wrong crowd, and then not showing up for a couple of days."

"Hum," Jean said. Which, when you think about it, was better than not saying anything at all.

Then she stood up and began clearing off the table and I took Johnny Mac upstairs to the playroom.

The playroom is on the second floor of our house and is this big windowed room that looks out over twin peaks straight into Tejas County at least twenty miles away. It's a real pretty view, no matter what the weather, and right then the weather was about as nice as it could get. It was late April and almost everything was in bloom and greening up really nice. Being a Yankee, my wife was into bulb flowers, and from all the windows in that second-floor room Johnny Mac and I could look down on the new buds of irises, crocuses, tulips and the like. They'd sizzle up in the heat of an Oklahoma summer, but Jean never stopped trying to bring a little Midwest to her new home.

The room itself is comfortable with an oversized sofa and chairs, little beanbag chairs that just fit Johnny Mac, and lots of toy baskets, although the toys were rarely actually in the baskets—more like scattered around the room. Johnny Mac's plastic indoor slide and jungle gym were in the playroom, along with an old TV and VCR and his favorite tapes, an old record player and his kid records, and the like.

I sat in an old rocker and watched my son play, trying not to think about my first time in this room, when the house had belonged to Laura Johnson, and we'd sat up here while her kids were away and watched a storm work its way toward us from Tejas County.

I tried not to think about that at all, because seeing it then in my mind's eye and seeing the room now, with my little boy playing in it—well, it just seemed to me that if the Supreme Court still needed a definition of obscenity, I could surely now explain it to them. Because it was obscene to think of this room where my son played so innocently and remember being in it with Laura Johnson.

I love my wife. I have a passion for her. I can see her across a room when I don't expect to and get hot for her, right then and there. Jean McDonnell is a beautiful, sexy woman and the mother of my only child. She's my wife and my friend and my roommate, and the person I like the most in the whole world.

So how come I was sitting up in the windowed room, half watching my boy play with his trucks, and mostly thinking about another woman? What had it been about Laura Johnson—what was it still—that grabbed my gut and wouldn't let it go? She'd hurt me just about as bad as one person can hurt another one. Maybe that was it. When something ends that bad, the scars run pretty deep, I guess.

But a hell of a lot had happened to me in the eleven years since I last set eyes on Laura Johnson. Those scars should have scabbed over and healed new a long time ago.

I tried to concentrate on what she'd said, rather than on the fact that she'd said anything at all. Try not to think about who she is, my official self kept saying. It's a problem. Just concentrate on that.

Trent Johnson Marshall, (his new name, as I understood the new husband had adopted all three kids) age eighteen, had started hanging out with what his mother termed a bunch of old hippies and computer freaks at a house near the outskirts of Lydecker, county seat of Tejas County, where the mother and her children now lived with her new husband, Dixon Marshall. According to the mother, Trent and his girlfriend, Amanda Nederwald, had left the house in the company of some of these hippie/computer types and gone on a retreat somewhere in Prophesy County. My county. After a couple of days the mother (not Laura, I told myself. Just the mother. The mother of the alleged victim) went over to the house and found most of the inhabitants there—except for Trent and Amanda. When asked, she was told the two had decided to stay on at the retreat. When she asked for the phone number of the retreat, they said they didn't have the number. When she asked about the location, she was given a vague and generalized area.

Laura Johnson (now Marshall) and her family lived in Tejas County. The last time I'd seen her, I'd told her to go home to Lubbock, Texas, but it looked like she hadn't made it that far. She was living only one county over, a county I could actually see out of the windows of the second-floor playroom. A county I went to on business once or twice a month. A place I used to feel safe in. Not anymore. Not now that I knew Laura Johnson was there.

Think about the problem, I told myself. The problem.

The mother had gone to the authorities in her county—my friend Bill Williams—and he'd told her there wasn't anything he could do about it as the boy was eighteen and the retreat was in Prophesy County, which was my jurisdiction. Bill had suggested the mother call me. Bill didn't know the history, so I couldn't blame him, much as I wanted to.

There were a couple of things I could do. I should probably call Bill Williams, see what he could tell me about the people Trent had been with in his county who had taken the kids to the retreat, call the office and see where exactly in my county this so-called retreat was, and maybe get my second-in-command, Emmett Hopkins, to do what had to be done.

When you think about it, there was no reason really for me to get involved. I was the high sheriff. I should be acting like my predecessor, Elberry Blankenship, best sheriff the county ever had, and start some serious delegating. No reason I had to dirty my hands with this at all. The mother had called me because Bill Williams had suggested it, and because of a past history. That I had to admit. But there was no reason I had to take this on my own self. Not when I had delegating capabilities close at hand.

I picked up the phone in the playroom and called Emmett at his house.

"You got anything on your plate?" I asked him after he answered the phone.

"Been working that car-jacking in Bishop and that string of burglaries over in the southeast."

"Right." I'd forgotten about both of them. What should I do—suggest Emmett give one or both of those cases over to Dalton Pettigrew—my only other day deputy—a man who couldn't find his own butt with both hands, a flashlight, and a glow-in-the-dark map? Move Jasmine to days so she could help out—except she was working that so-called streetwalker ring (we think there were two of them) working out of the Dew Drop Inn out on Highway 5. My other night deputy, Hank Dobbins, was up in Tulsa taking a course and would be gone for another week or more.

"Okay," I finally said. "Never mind."

"What's the problem, Milt?" Emmett asked. Emmett was my closest guy friend, and we asked each other questions like that sometimes, although we both tried real hard never to answer truthfully.

"No big deal," I said. "Just got a complaint that might need some legwork. I'll handle it."

"Well, hopefully I can clear up one of these by the end of the week—" he started.

"If I still need you then, I'll let you know."

"You watching the game tomorrow?" Emmett asked.

"Is a pig's ass pork? You wanna come over?"

"I'll bring the beer," he said.

"None of that lite shit," I suggested.

"Hell, man, if I wanted to drink piss, we could just wring out one of Johnny Mac's diapers!"

We both laughed in a manly way and rang off.

Now I was gonna have to deal with Laura on my own. Part of me felt sick at the idea; another part felt kind of excited. That's the part that scared the bejesus out of me.

The retreat, called the Seven Trumpets, was located in the northwest corner of the county, not too far from the Tejas County line. Nobody seemed to know much about them, other than the fact that it was listed as a church in the tax records, had a couple of satellite dishes, and used a lot more

11

electricity and had a lot more telephone lines than the average church.

I called Bill Williams in Tejas County and asked him what he knew about the problem.

"Only what the mother told me, Milt," he said. "I went on over to the house he'd been hanging out at and talked to some of the people there, but they didn't know much. And hell, Milt, the boy's eighteen."

"The mother said something about kidnapping," I said.

Bill laughed. "Yeah, well, you know how women are. I think this is a case of a mama not wanting to cut the apron strings."

"Who'd you talk to at that house?" I asked him.

I heard Bill shuffling papers, then he said, "Naomi Woman."

"Excuse me?"

Bill laughed. "That's what she said. Naomi Woman, and she ain't even an Indian. Some white girl with a dumb name."

"Think she made it up?" I asked.

"You think the pope's Polish?" Bill asked.

"You run her?" I asked.

Bill sighed. "Milt, got no reason to. She's got a funny name. Not against the law in this county."

"What she say about the boy? Trent?"

"A bunch of them went to the retreat in your county"—I could hear rustling paper again—"something called the Seven Trumpets. Stayed there for the weekend, and then, when they came back, the boy and his girlfriend, this Amanda Nederwald, decided to stay on. Now I did call Amanda Nederwald's people, her mama and stepdaddy over to Mooney, and her mama told me Amanda called her from the retreat and said she'd be staying on for a while and could her momma send her some cash. Her momma said she sent her twenty dollars care of general delivery in Bishop."

"You got a telephone number for this Naomi Woman?" I asked.

Bill rattled off a number, and I said, "You mind me calling her? Maybe going by the house and see how the land lies?"

"Well, call all you want, Milt. But if you come into my county on business, I'd appreciate you letting me know you're here. Maybe I'll go out there with you."

"Will do, Bill. Thanks for your time."

I rang off and stared at the number he had given me. And I thought that probably Bill was right. Laura was overreacting. I remembered how she was about her kids, her crazy, obsessive behavior. It fit with what I remembered. The boy was eighteen. The girl's family didn't seem all that fired up.

But there was something else nagging at me. I didn't know diddly about this retreat—this Seven Trumpets. And I didn't like the thought of some nutcase harboring runaway teenagers in my county. Even if the teenagers were of age. Something smelled, and for a change it wasn't Johnny Mac's diaper.

Naomi Woman had a voice like Minnie Mouse—kind of high and squeaky. By talking to her on the phone, I figured her to be anywhere from twelve to sixty. It's hard to tell with that kind of voice.

I identified myself and told her Bill Williams had given me her number.

"Oh, well, this must be about Trent and Amanda," she said.

"Yes, ma'am," I said. "I just talked to Mrs. Marshall—"

Naomi Woman laughed. "Oh, we all know about Mrs. Marshall! She calls here all the time, and has ever since Trent started hanging out here. Half the time now we screen the calls so we won't have to talk to her."

"Well, the lady's worried about her boy, ma'am," I said.

"Okay, fine, except Trent's not a boy, and to hear him tell it, she worries a little more than she should."

Personally, I didn't want to get in the position of defending Laura's mothering skills, so I said, "Can you tell me why Trent and Amanda didn't come back with y'all from the retreat last weekend?"

"We were packing up the van and I was told Trent and Amanda wouldn't be returning with us."

"Who told you that, ma'am?"

"Brother Grigsby told me."

"Okay," I said, "and who is Brother Grigsby?"

"Brother Grigsby, Sheriff," Naomi Woman said, like she was talking to a slow two-year-old, "the spiritual leader of the Seven Trumpets." Her voice took on a breathy quality.

"You didn't see Trent and Amanda when you left?" I asked.

"No, Brother Grigsby told us they wanted to stay. We figured that was their choice. They're both adults, Sheriff."

"How come you told Mrs. Marshall there wasn't a phone at this retreat? According to my records, there are a bunch of phone lines there."

"Because I didn't want that woman calling up and harassing Brother Grigsby," she said. "Now is there anything else I can do for you, Sheriff?" Naomi Woman asked, her voice taking on a not so nice quality.

"I'm looking for Trent Marshall and Amanda Nederwald, ma'am."

"To the best of my knowledge, they are still at the retreat, receiving spiritual purification from the blessed Source himself, Brother Grigsby."

"Uh-huh," I said. "Well, thank you, ma'am." I rang off.

Now I'm a card-carrying member of the First Baptist Church of Longbranch, and I even go on occasion, but I got to admit I've never had my spirit purified. It sounded a little painful to

14

me, but then I've been called a heathen in my time, although mostly by my first wife, LaDonna, who seems to have the market cornered on knowing all about heathens, communists, liberals, and deviants. Somehow, on more than one occasion in our twenty-year marriage, I managed to end up in all those categories—sometimes simultaneously.

But all in all, I wasn't real happy with what I'd found out from Naomi Woman. It looked to me like maybe I'd better take a drive up to the northeast corner of the county and check out the source, so to speak.

There's a lot of pine and oak in the northeast section of Prophesy County, not to mention a bit of mesquite, too. Except for making rifle stocks and burning it in a barbecue pit, God never did come up with a good reason for mesquite, I figured. Just a prickly old tree without enough shade to cool off a gnat. When I was about fourteen, me and my best friend Lin Robinson got lost in a mesquite woods just south of Bishop. By the time we made the highway, we were cut to ribbons from those prickly trees and I swore I would never get up close and personal with a mesquite again.

From what I could see once I reached the closed gate of the Seven Trumpets, the expensive hurricane fencing was doing nothing more than keeping in a nasty old forest of mesquite trees. There was a dirt road leading into the land, cut off by a padlocked gate and a cattle guard that had tire-gouging barbs sticking up out of it, and that was certainly a deterrent to moving my Jeep Cherokee through.

I got out of the car and walked up to the fence. Cattle were grazing not too far away and I could make out the brand— the Circle L, big as life. The Leventhwart brand. Having been part of the Leventhwart family for more years than I care to admit—by marriage, not blood, thank God—I recognized the brand and it finally came to me where I was. I'd just come up on the land from the back way, which is probably why I didn't recognize it. Bert Leventhwart had been my brother-in-law, LaDonna's oldest brother, and my boss for ten of the twenty years I was married to his sister. I was a salesman in one of Bert's used-car lots; I wasn't very good at it, but Bert was a born used-car salesman. Which should tell you something about Bert. Seemed like in some strange way, all my women were coming back to haunt me. Not a pleasant thought.

I looked over the hurricane fencing—something Bert had never put out the bucks for, I can guaran-damn-tee you that— and saw movement over by a scrub oak a couple of hundred yards off.

There was a bull standing under the scrub oak and some-thing just beyond him. At first I couldn't figure out what it was, but then one of the vultures moved. There was something lying in front of the bull. The bull was a longhorn, old and scrawny, but with horns to reckon with.

Squinting, I thought I could make out an arm or a leg, something human-looking, anyway. Or formerly human.

I scrambled up the side of the hurricane fence, taking a lot longer than I would have twenty years ago (which was prob-ably the last time I tried anything that foolish), and fell over to the other side. I got up and stood there for a minute, trying to figure out what to do about that bull. Scrawny and old he might be, I thought, but that didn't mean he couldn't drive one of those long horns of his through my gut.

I took my jacket off and held it loosely in my left hand, away from my body, toreador-style, and walked slowly toward the scrub oak tree.

The bull jerked his head up as I approached and gave me the evil eye. He snorted, a fine spray of snot blowing out of his nose. I stopped. He stared at me a full minute, then bent

16

his head back to feeding on the new sprouts of grass under the tree. I took a few more steps. I could definitely see the thing under the tree now. It was a body all right, a female, naked as the day she was born, long blond hair entwined on the hooklike feet of a vulture.

I had a choice now, but not a very good one. I could shoo the vultures off the body, but that would probably agitate the bull. Or I could go back to the Jeep and call in for assistance, leaving the poor girl's body to the not so gentle ministrations of the vultures. I like to think of myself as a manly man.

So I ran toward the vultures flopping my arms and yelling.

The good news was they flew right off; the bad news was that the old bull didn't like that one little bit and charged me.

I managed to throw my jacket over his face, momentarily blinding him, and ran for the scrub oak, jumping up and grabbing a low-hanging tree limb.

I'm not a young man, nor am I a fit and skinny man. Actually, I'm looking the barrel of sixty right in the eye, I'm overweight, and prone to resting a great deal. I did manage to grab a tree limb, but I was heavier than it was and we both ended up on the ground, the limb managing to hit me on the head on its way down.

Now I do believe if a bull could laugh, that one would have been having a grand old time. Since he couldn't, he just walked off to a less occupied grazing spot and ignored me totally.

I got up and dusted my britches off, then headed for the girl's body. She was a mess, but I couldn't tell what was caused by the buzzards and what had actually killed her. I found my jacket the bull had discarded and placed it over the body, then walked back to the fence and the Jeep.

Time for some backup.

2

Emmett pulled up in a squad car driven by Dalton Pettigrew. By this time I was back on the other side of the fence, trying to keep the vultures off the body and the bull off me.

I hollered at Dalton, "Get on the phone and find a number for this so-called retreat and get somebody from there out here. We can't drive in 'cause of the barbs. Emmett, come on out here with me."

I was happy to see Emmett had as hard a time getting over the fence as I had, but he did it and came out to where the body lay, keeping one eye on the old bull.

"Whatja got, Milt?" he asked.

"Dead girl, looks like," I said. "Matches the description of the girl run off with the Marshall boy, but then again, lots of blondes in the county. Could be more than one out here."

"Reckon," Emmett said, pulling a stick of Juicy Fruit out of his shirt pocket and offering me one. I accepted. Juicy Fruit has an odor that can help block out the smell of death.

"Milt?" Dalton hollered over the fence.

"Yeah, Dalton?" I called, knowing he wouldn't go on unless I acknowledged him.

"Got hold somebody up yonder," he said, pointing toward the road that led into the compound. "Somebody's coming."

"Good work, Dalton. You stay there and mind the radio."

"Okay, Milt."

"Whatja think kilt her?" Emmett asked, staring down at the girl, now uncovered by my ruined jacket.

"Gonna have to have Dr. Jim come out and look at her." I hollered at Dalton, "You call Dr. Jim yet?"

"Uh, was I s'pose' to?"

I sighed. I hadn't told him to do it. We do it every time there's a dead body, but I hadn't specifically told him to do it this time. "Yeah, Dalton, go ahead and call Dr. Jim. Get him on over here."

"Okay, Milt," he said, sliding his big frame behind the wheel and going for the radio. He wouldn't be able to get Dr. Jim on the radio; he'd have to use the cell phone, but I knew he'd figure that out eventually.

"Interesting," Emmett said, nodding his head at something behind me. I turned to see. A man was riding up on a bicycle.

Jean had made me watch a movie she rented not too long ago. It was a good enough movie, I guess, no car chases or anything, but it was interesting. About this guy Gandhi who was a big deal in India a while back. The guy on the bicycle was wearing an outfit just like Gandhi wore, when Gandhi wasn't running around half-naked, that is. It was white, a big loose top over loose-fitting baggy pants, both out of the same homespun-looking material. The guy on the bike was bald as an egg and wore a huge silver medallion around his neck.

It wasn't until he got off the bike and walked toward me that I recognized him. Barry Leventhwart, my ex-nephew-in-law.

"Hey, Barry," I said, sticking out my hand to shake.

Instead of shaking it, Barry clasped his hands together in

19

front of him as if he was praying and bowed at the waist.

When he straightened up, he grinned at me. "Hey, Milt, how you?"

"Can't complain. Do got a problem, though," I said, moving away from the dead body so he could see behind me.

"Oh, sweet Jesus!" Barry said, dropping down beside the body.

I grabbed an arm. "Don't touch anything, Barry. This is a crime scene."

"It's Amanda!" he said. He looked up at me. "My God, what happened?"

"We're not sure yet. Dr. Jim's on his way. Some of the damage was done by vultures, so we're not sure what mighta killed her. Can you tell me the last time you saw the girl?"

Barry stood up, his body shaking. "Ah, jeez, Milt. Let me think. Ah, yesterday. Or last night, really. Her and her boy-friend left the compound right after lights-out. Brother Grigsby sent me to talk to them as they were leaving, but the boy, Trent, wasn't having any of it. He said they were leaving. We're not a prison here, Milt," he said, a bit defensively, I thought. "I just let 'em go."

"I'm gonna need to talk to this Brother Grigsby," I said.

Barry shook his head. "Sorry, Milt. No can do. Brother Grigsby only speaks to people of the order."

"Pardon?" I said, not quite believing what I'd just heard.

Barry continued to shake his head. "He only speaks to the anointed, Milt. He must stay clean."

Well, now. I took a shower that morning and was about to say so, but thought that probably wasn't what Barry was re-ferring to. Emmett looked at me and we both rolled our eyes.

"It can't be helped, Barry," I said. "He's gonna have to talk to us."

Barry put his hands together again in that prayerlike posture, and spoke to me like I wouldn't speak to Johnny Mac. "You must understand, Sheriff, that Brother Grigsby is not of this world."

"What? He some kind of alien?" Emmett asked.

Barry ignored him. "Brother Grigsby is on a higher plane than mere mortals, Sheriff. I am his emissary here on earth and I must be the one to handle this problem."

He bowed from the waist again, then let his hands drop to his side. He smiled a syrupy little smile.

"Your mama and daddy know what you're doing with this land?" I asked.

"This land belongs to the Holy Temple of Seven Trumpets in the person of our source, Brother Grigsby. The people of my past have no claim on me or this land."

I couldn't help snickering inside, knowing how seriously pissed off this would make my ex-brother-in-law, Bert. He wouldn't so much mind losing a son as he would losing this nice parcel of land right on the river. I'm sure Bert's vision of condos lost kept him up late at night.

"We're gonna need to go down to the compound," I said.

"The nonanointed aren't allowed in the compound, Sheriff. Actually, having you on this land at all is a blasphemy." He grinned the old Leventhwart grin. "If you were anybody else, I'd be calling the sheriff right now to have you arrested for trespass."

I could feel Emmett bristling up beside me. Emmett used to be chief of police of Longbranch, the county seat of Prophesy County, and only came to work with me when city politics got to be a little too much for him. County politics sucks too, but as head investigator, not head cop, he doesn't have to deal with the powers that be the way I do.

I put a hand on Emmett's chest, a warning to him to calm himself down a mite.

I smiled at Barry. It was the smile my wife calls the cat that ate the canary one. I used to call it my shit-eating grin, but then Jean's got a lot more class than I have. "Here's the thing, Barry. This is a crime scene. Looks like this young lady here's been murdered. Until I know for sure one way or the other, I have to treat it as such. So, here's the thing. I either go up to your compound and talk to some people, his royal heinie included, or I arrest your ass for obstructing justice, take you to town and go to the bother of getting a search warrant so I can come back here with about a dozen deputies and go over this compound with a fine-toothed comb, and still manage to get me my interview with your source fella." I smiled bigger. "Take your pick. The easy way or the hard way?"

"My daddy always did say you were a son of a bitch," Barry said.

"Now, you can call me a prick, you can me an asshole, but don't be saying mean things about my mama, God rest her soul. We going up there now, Barry, or we fitting you for a new outfit down at the jailhouse?"

Barry sighed, took a tool and some keys out of one of the deep pockets of his fancy pants, and walked over to the driveway to the gate. He unlocked the padlock and opened the gate, then bent down to where the barbs stuck out of the cattle guard. He fiddled with something under the cattle guard, and the barbs went away.

"Mind if I put my bike in the back of your Jeep?" he asked.

"Not a bit," I said, walking to my Jeep and opening the tailgate for Barry to put the bike in.

"Dalton, you go over there and wait for Dr. Jim. Keep the vultures off the body," I said, pointing at the tree in case Dalton hadn't yet figured out what was going on. "Tell him to take the body when he's ready and I'll call him later."

Dalton nodded his head up and down. "Wait for Doc over

yonder," he said, pointing where I had pointed. "Then tell him to take the body and you'll call him?"

"That's right, Dalton," I said.

He grinned. "Okay, Milt. Gotja!"

I sighed and climbed behind the wheel of the Jeep, Emmett sliding in the shotgun side, leaving the back for my ex-nephew-in-law.

The compound consisted of what appeared to be a hastily put together building that I couldn't see withstanding an Oklahoma winter. It was made out of whitewashed plywood with an aluminum roof. A pavilion of sorts stuck out from the front of it, with long tables and folding chairs under it. In the distance I could see a couple of very large tents and two trailers—one an old aluminum-sided Airstream, the other a fancy new double-wide. All the buildings, the tent included, had jerry-rigged onion-looking domes sitting on top, all painted a glaring gold.

I looked down at the ground and saw red Oklahoma clay; the trees were oaks and scrub pine with a smattering of mesquite. Yeah, I was still in Oklahoma, despite the looks of the place.

Two women stood by one of the posts holding up the pavilion. Both were dressed just like Barry, in white homespun-looking top and pants, but both had long hair hanging in one long braid down their backs, the tops of their heads covered with white kerchiefs tied behind the braid. The tall one wore a medallion like Barry's, same size, only it was gold instead of silver. The shorter one wore a silver medallion just like Barry's and had a poochy-out stomach that made me think she might be pregnant. As we got out of the Jeep, both held their hands together like Barry had done and bowed from the waist.

"Brother Barry," said the taller woman, a wispy-looking

23

dishwater-blonde with pale skin and blue eyes so pale she looked like the cartoon strip *Little Orphan Annie*. "You have brought strangers into the compound?"

"Sorry, Sister Alma. Couldn't help it. I got real bad news. Little Sister Amanda's dead."

Both women gasped, then bowed their heads, hands clasped in front of them. "Dear Lord our Saviour, our Source of light and inspiration," said Sister Alma, "we beseech you, take our fallen sister into your loving arms so that she may wander unencumbered on the other side."

Both women looked up then. I didn't hear an "amen," but I guess that was just sorta assumed.

"I'm Sheriff Milt Kovak," I said to Sister Alma. "I'm gonna need to talk to Brother Grigsby. And may I ask, is that his first or last name?" I took out my notebook to write it down.

The two women looked at each other. Then Sister Alma looked at Barry. "Brother Barry, may the Lord forgive you for blaspheming. You must escort these gentlemen off the grounds before Brother Grigsby feels their presence."

Oh, goody, I thought. Now the guy can feel our presence. I decided I really had to meet this character.

"Like I told Barry, Miss Alma," I said, deciding to do away with all the brother/sister crap, "we are investigating what looks like a murder. This whole compound is part of a crime scene. Therefore we gotta interview everybody in this place, and that includes Mr. Grigsby."

The woman stood up straighter, her shoulders braced. "Sheriff, this is a religious retreat and you are stepping on our First Amendment rights."

"A murder investigation supercedes your First Amendment rights," I said, wondering if I'd have to contact our county attorney to find out if I was anywhere near right on that. Hoping Sister Alma hadn't been a lawyer in her previous life,

I went on. "I can go get a warrant, but then I'd be coming back here with a whole parcel of deputies to go over this compound with a fine-toothed comb," I said, just like I'd threatened Barry earlier. Counting Emmett and Dalton, both already here, my force of deputies included four. And not one of us had a fine-toothed comb, but I was betting none of these people knew that.

"I protest strongly," Sister Alma said.

I nodded my head. "Your protest is duly noted," I said, writing that down in my notebook, sorta making it look official. "Now, if you wouldn't mind, I'd like to speak to Mr. Grigsby."

Sister Alma sighed. The smaller woman, who hadn't been introduced, snuck a look at the taller woman, and I coulda sworn the little lady had fear in her eyes.

Yeah, I was really looking forward to meeting old Brother Grigsby.

They had me and Emmett wait in the main building. It looked to be a sanctuary, with a podium at the front and mean, backless benches in rows. There was a wall with two doors behind the podium, dividing the big room. We sat on benches toward the back and waited, neither of us saying much.

Finally, the door to the far left opened and a man came out. I'm not sure what I expected, maybe one of those guru-looking guys the Beatles used to hang out with or something like that. What I didn't expect is what I got. A tall, painfully skinny guy wearing well-worn blue jeans and a chambray work shirt. He had a nice healthy mustache, the likes of which I haven't seen since the sixties, and longish dark brown hair that curled around his ears. The only thing he wore that resembled the others was the large gold medallion around his neck. The thing he wore that least resembled the others was a great big old smile.

"Sheriff Kovak," he said, walking toward me and sticking out his hand. "It's nice to finally meet you." The smile faded. "I just wish it had been under less tragic circumstances."

I stood and shook his hand. "Brother Grigsby," I said. "Nice to meet you, too." Emmett stood next to me and I introduced him. The two men shook hands, then Brother Grigsby sat down on the bench in front of the one we'd been using. Emmett and I sat down opposite him.

"This is such a shock," Brother Grigsby said, shaking his head. "Sister Amanda was a really special person. She was going to be a great blessing to our flock."

"I thought Barry said her and her boyfriend were leaving last night?"

Brother Grigsby sighed. "That's true, but I think that had more to do with the Marshall boy than it did with Amanda. I'm afraid Trent wasn't as happy here as we'd hoped." He sighed again. "Humanist jealousy rearing its ugly head."

"Jealous of what?" I asked.

Brother Grigsby shrugged. "Sharing. Sharing Amanda's love. We believe in total brotherhood here at Seven Trumpets, Sheriff. We eat communally, we work communally, we sleep communally."

"Does that mean he didn't want the rest of you having sex with his girlfriend?" Emmett asked, a little more direct than I might have been, but at least he got to the point.

Brother Grigsby laughed. "Oh, orgies? Is that what you think? I'm sorry if I led you to believe that," he said. "See those tents over there?" he said, pointing.

We nodded.

"Those are the dorms. And no, men and women do not comingle here. Which I think was part of Trent's problem."

26

Brother Grigsby sighed again. "I'm afraid there's a great possibility that Trent had had carnal knowledge of poor Amanda before they came to us. Here, of course, we do not indulge in sins of the flesh."

Which made me wonder how the shorter woman out front happened to be so pregnant.

"I coulda sworn I saw a pregnant woman outside," Emmett said, reading my thoughts, although I hadn't actually wanted to go there yet. I was afraid I was gonna have to have a talk with Emmett about who was in charge. Though, of course, that could wait a while.

Grigsby smiled. "Sister Ruth is a married woman. She is Brother Barry's wife."

"So it's okay for married couples—" I started.

Grigsby rolled his eyes. "Of course, Sheriff." He laughed. "We are a Christian community. We believe strongly in family."

I nodded. "Okay, let's get down to some basics here, Brother Grigsby. I need to know your full name."

"Theodore Davis Grigsby."

"And where're you from originally?"

Grigsby smiled. "I was first born in Cleveland, Ohio, Sheriff, to mortal woman. I was reborn in Christ in a small town in Colorado fifteen years ago."

"Uh-huh," I said. Whatever. "And the other members of your, ah, flock?"

Grigsby threw his head back and laughed. "Where do I start?"

"How about Sister Alma?" I suggested.

He smiled. "My wife," he said. "We met in that small town in Colorado I mentioned, fifteen years ago. Who she was before that I do not know, nor do I care. She is my wife and has been for almost five years. That's all that matters."

To you maybe, I thought. "Her maiden name?" I asked.

He smiled. "You'd have to ask her."

I looked at Emmett out of the corner of my eye. He was suppressing something, either a need to laugh or a need to knock this guy's block off.

"And Sister ah, Ruth, you said?"

"Brother Barry's wife."

"Maiden name?"

Again he smiled, shaking his head. "You'd have to ask her."

I decided to switch tactics. "How many people you got living here?" I asked. "I didn't see anybody but the three outside."

"We've had as many as a hundred, but it varies. A little less than that now."

"So where are they all?" I asked.

"We toil, Sheriff. In the fields and in town."

"So they're all off working?"

"That's right."

"Were they all around last night when Trent and Amanda left?"

"Most were. We have evening services before lights-out. All those who do not work in town at night come to evening services."

"So we'll need to interview these people," I said.

"I don't mean to tell you your business, Sheriff, but why bother my flock when all you need to do is find Trent? Obviously, and may God forgive me for saying so, but Trent must have killed Amanda."

I sighed and thanked the good Brother Grigsby in my heart of hearts for finally putting into words what I didn't even want to think about. "What makes you think that?" I asked.

"They left together, Sheriff. Brother Barry saw them leaving. He told me and I asked him to have a word with them. He

28

reported back to me later that Trent was adamant that they leave. It appeared to him at the time, as he told me, that Amanda was not as adamant. I do believe she wanted to stay. Which makes me think that might be the reason he wanted to leave. It stands to reason that someone of Trent's temperament might try to demand a, shall we say, return engagement?"

I wondered then if Brother Grigsby knew about Trent's daddy. And if he wasn't insinuating that the apple doesn't fall far from the tree. The thought had passed my mind, too, though I didn't want to dwell on it. When your daddy's a convicted rapist and murderer, does that mean you're gonna be one, too?

"That's a lot of speculation, Brother Grigsby, with no facts to back it up. Our ME will find out if the girl was raped, and if she was and they didn't use a condom, we'll know pretty quick who did it. Meanwhile, I'm gonna need to interview your people that were here last night."

Brother Grigsby nodded. "The ones who toil the fields I'll bring in one at a time now," he said. "The ones who work in town will have to be interviewed this evening."

I nodded my head. The interviews of the field-workers could take a while, I thought, which meant putting off the phone call to Laura. And that was something I dearly wanted to put off.

29

3

I left the interviewing to Emmett and headed back to town. I needed to see Dr. Jim, and phone calls had to be made. I needed to call Amanda's mother and, at some point, I needed to call Laura.

Amanda Nederwald's body was the only one in the morgue. We'd had a wreck on the highway recently, with three teenagers and an old man doing a head-on. The old man lived, but all three teens had ended up in Dr. Jim's office. But all three had been buried the day before, leaving the morgue empty.

Dr. Jim had cleaned her up and you could tell she'd been a pretty girl in life. Long blond hair, blue eyes now opaque in death, and a pretty little figure, what hadn't been picked at by the buzzards.

"You figure cause of death, Dr. Jim?" I asked.

He looked at me like I was a slightly special two-year-old. "What am I? A magician?"

"Not so's I've noticed," I countered.

"Damn vultures did their work good. Can't hardly tell what's vulture-chomping and what's a knife, but I do believe there are some knife wounds here."

"That what killed her?" I asked.

"Boy, you just don't listen, do you?" Dr. Jim grumbled. "Can't hardly understand why a woman as smart as Jean McDonnell would hook up with the likes of you. I'll tell you all when I know all, okay, Sheriff?" he said, making my title sound like a dirty word.

"Was she raped?" I asked.

He sighed. "Jesus Christ on a bicycle. Get out of here 'fore I hit you with something hard."

"Call me," I said as I left the morgue. I heard something heavy hit the door behind me. Dr. Jim's got a real attitude.

I went back to my office and got on the phone. First I called Bill Williams and told him what had happened.

"Oh, Lord," he said. "That's awful, Milt. Just awful. But glad it was your county and not mine."

"You're all heart, Williams, you know that?"

"You want me to go with you to tell the mama?"

"I was planning on calling her," I said, my pulse racing and my skin paling at the thought of seeing Laura eye-to-eye.

"I think the girl's mama deserves a face-to-face, Milt," Bill said.

"Oh, that mama," I said, breathing easier. "Yeah, you're right. I'll be there in thirty."

The Nederwalds lived in a trailer park outside Lydecker. Their trailer was a single-wide that had seen better days. What once had been white over pink aluminum was now beige over darker beige, the aluminum steps decrepit, and neither Bill nor I had any desire to step on them.

Bill leaned forward from the ground to rap on the door of

the trailer. It was opened by a woman in cutoffs and a halter top. She didn't look more than thirty, thirty-five at the most, with bleached-blond hair and a baby on her hip.

"Yeah?" she said.

"Excuse me, ma'am," Bill said, "we're looking for Mrs. Nederwald. Amanda's mother."

"I'm Amanda's mother. But the name's Tatum. Becca Tatum. What's wrong?"

"I'm Sheriff Bill Williams of Tejas County and this is Sheriff Milt Kovak of Prophesy County."

"Oh, for God's sake!" she said, rolling her eyes, and moving back inside the trailer. "What's that girl gone and done now?"

Gingerly Bill and I went up the steps and entered the trailer. It was a mess. Toys were scattered everywhere, along with piles of dirty laundry and dirty dishes all over the kitchen. A boy about two was playing with a truck, making the same truck noises as my own boy, and a boy about ten lay in front of the TV, watching cartoons.

"May we talk to you privately, Miz Tatum?" Bill asked.

"Travis!" she yelled, the boy in front of the TV barely moving in response. "Travis! Turn off that goddamn TV and you and Tyler go outside. Take the baby with you."

The boy Travis got slowly up from the floor, taking the infant from his mother's arms. He hit the two-year-old on the back of the head as he went by. "Come on, stupid! Outside!"

"Don't call him stupid, you shithead!" his mother called as the three went out the door. She sighed. "Kids! You want one of 'em?" she said and laughed.

"Miz Tatum, about Amanda—" Bill started.

"Look, the girl's eighteen. I don't have no control over her anymore—like I ever did! That one's always had a mind of her own—"

"Ma'am," I said. "We got bad news."

32

She finally shut up. "What?"

"Ma'am, Amanda's body was found this morning—"

She screamed. A loud piercing scream that had the older boy flying in the front door of the trailer, fists raised as he headed toward Bill and me in an attempt to protect his mama.

He began pelting us with his fists and Bill was the first to get to him, grab his arms, and hold them down at his side. "It's okay, boy," he said.

"Oh, sweet Jesus!" Mrs. Tatum wailed. "Tell me she ain't dead!"

"I'm sorry, ma'am," I said. "but she is. Her body's at the morgue—"

She commenced screaming again, which started the boy up with the fists again. The two-year-old came in the door and headed into the ruckus, a stick in his hand that he used to whack me on the knee. I picked him up and removed the stick from his hands, while I wondered where the infant had gotten to and whether he'd be joining the ruckus soon.

I didn't have to wait long to wonder. A woman came barreling in the door, the infant on her hip, two smaller children following behind her and another woman behind them. "Becca! You okay? Hey, who are you guys!" Turning to the other woman, the first said, "Reba, go get your gun!"

"Hold it!" I said, putting the two-year-old down. "We're law, ladies, okay? We just brought Miz Tatum some bad news. Could y'all come in and help her?"

"What bad news?" the first woman demanded.

Mrs. Tatum threw her arms around the woman's neck. "Oh, Clarisse! It's my baby girl! It's my Amanda! She's dead!"

Clarisse dropped the grieving mother like a hot potato. "Dead?" she said, standing and staring at Bill and me, hands on her hips. "Car wreck?" she demanded.

"No, ma'am," I said. "It looks like foul play at the moment."

"Ha! I knew it!" Clarisse said. "That Marshall boy! Becca, didn't I tell you her messing with that high-faluting Marshall boy was gonna come to no good? Didn't I tell you?"

Mrs. Tatum jumped up and grabbed Bill by the lapels. "Did he do something to my Amanda? Did he? Did he kill my Amanda?"

"Ma'am, we're not sure what happened yet. It's still an open investigation. But we'll let you know—"

"Don't you let them Marshalls run roughshod over this!" she screamed. "They gonna try to cover up shit and you don't let 'em, you hear me?"

"Ma'am, can we call your husband to come—"

"Fat lot of good that fool's gonna do anybody!" Clarisse said.

Becca Tatum shook her head. "We're separated. He weren't Amanda's daddy anyway. He never did like her much."

She went and picked the infant out of Reba's arms. Nuzzling the baby's neck, she began to cry softly. "My sweet babies. All my sweet babies! Oh, Lord, Lord, Lord."

Bill and I headed for the front door. "We'll be in touch, Miz Tatum," I said, walking out the door. I tripped going down the steps and landed on one knee, but nobody inside seemed to notice. Bill got me on my feet and we headed as fast as we could to his squad car.

Bill decided his next stop would be at the Marshalls'. I wasn't all that thrilled about going there, but I figured I couldn't say much.

Laura had gone up in the world. The house on Falls Road where Laura had lived when I first met her, the one where I now lived with my wife and child, was nice enough, but didn't hold a candle to this Tara-look-alike.

Bill rang the doorbell and I stayed back a bit. I noticed my heart was thumping like mad and, much as I tried to quiet it down, it didn't seem to be having any of it.

The door was opened by a man and half of me sighed with gratitude while the other half started getting pissed.

"Mr. Marshall?" Bill said.

He was a tall, skinny old guy, a good twenty years older than Laura, one of those skinny old men who, when they gain weight, carry it all in their belly like a seven-month-pregnant woman. His worn jeans rode below the belly, his shirt was Western-cut, and his face was tanned and lined like leather, testifying to more than a few years of working out-of-doors.

"Yes, sir," Dixon Marshall answered. "And you are?"

"Sheriff Bill Williams of Tejas County. This here is Sheriff Milt Kovak of Prophi—"

"Milt!" a voice called from inside the house and then, there she was. Laura Johnson, in the flesh.

She looked the same. More gray in the jet-black hair, more lines on her freckled face. But the same. Turquoise eyes flashing. Beautiful in a way no other woman was. The sexiest woman I'd ever seen in the flesh.

When I knew her she was a lot younger and dressed like a housewife with three little kids—jeans and big T-shirts, hair windblown, face free of makeup.

Now, however, she was dressed like a woman of her station in life—that of the wife of a rich man. The pants were casual but looked more like linen than denim and the shirt was no longer an oversized man's shirt, but a silk blouse with a gold pin on the shoulder. A string of pearls was at her neck.

She held on to her husband's arm and looked out at me. "Milt! Have you heard anything about Trent?"

"Is that what this is about?" Dixon Marshall said, giving his wife a smile and patting her hand. "Honey, I told you. The boy's got some wild oats to sow, that's all."

35

"May we come in, Mr. Marshall?" Bill asked, hat in hand like he'd just come out of the field to the big house.

"Surely," Marshall said, ushering us inside.

Laura grabbed my arm. Carefully I extracted myself from her grasp. Didn't want to go touching Laura Johnson. No, I surely didn't.

Marshall led us into a beautifully appointed living room, very formal, very not the Laura I used to know. We sat down on brocade sofas and chairs, Laura perching lightly on the arm of her husband's chair.

"Milt, what have you heard?" she demanded.

"I need to ask a few questions first, Mrs. Marshall," I said, keeping myself as businesslike as I could.

"No need for the 'Mrs.' stuff, Sheriff," Dixon Marshall said. "I know you and my wife have a history. Might as well call her Laura."

I could feel Bill Williams giving me a look, but I let it slide. I also let what Dixon Marshall said slide, too.

"Have y'all heard from Trent since we spoke?" I asked, looking at Laura for an answer.

"No, not a word! Did you talk to those weirdos he was hanging out with? Or go to that so-called retreat?"

"Here's the thing, Mr. Marshall, Mrs. Marshall," I said. "You know Amanda Nederwald, Trent's girlfriend?"

Laura got a prissy look on her face I'd never seen before. "I wouldn't call her his girlfriend, Milt. They were barely even friends, really," she said.

"Honey, let's call a spade a spade," Dixon Marshall said. "What about her, Sheriff?"

"I found her body this morning out at the Seven Trumpets—that retreat the two had gone to. She's dead. Looks like foul play."

36

Laura jumped up. "Oh my God! Where's Trent? Has he been hurt, too? Oh my God!"

Marshall stood and took his wife in his arms. "Hold on, honey. Just hold on." To me, he said, "What's the word on the boy, Sheriff?"

"The last we know he and Amanda were leaving the retreat last night. The people there said he was upset and wanted to leave. Nobody's seen him since."

Laura was trembling all over. "He's dead! They killed them both! Oh my God!"

Marshall's grip on his wife tightened. "Hold on, girl. Sheriff. What do you know so far?"

"The girl's down at the morgue being autopsied as we speak. My people are interviewing the other members of this retreat, see if we can find anybody who's seen Trent since last night."

"I want an APB put out on my son!"

"Ma'am," Bill Williams said, more deferential than I'd ever seen him, "I already told Sheriff Kovak he can have the use of any of my deputies to help look for the boy. We'll find him, don't you worry."

Dixon Marshall looked me straight in the eye. "You're thinking Trent might be mixed up in this girl's death?"

"She was just trash!" Laura spat. "Pure trailer trash! God only knows how many men she'd been with—now she probably deserved whatever—"

"Stop it!" Dixon Marshall said. "Have you told the girl's mama?" he asked me.

"Yes, sir," I said, beginning to like Dixon Marshall in spite of myself. "She took it pretty hard."

He put his hands on his wife's arms, turning her toward him. "Go get Hildy to take something out of the freezer to fix up for the mama. We need to take something to 'em." Laura stiffened. "Do it," he said, his tone brooking no argument.

37

I had a fleeting thought about trying to talk to my wife like that, then thinking about what I'd do when I woke up from my coma.

Laura shot a look at me, then headed out of the room.

"My wife's a bit upset, as you can well understand," Marshall said, sitting down on the brocade chair.

Bill and I followed suit on the matching sofa.

"What are they saying up at the retreat?" he asked.

"Just what I told you. That they haven't seen Trent since last night." No need, I thought, to go into idle speculation on the part of the good Brother Grigsby. "We may get more information from the other members. My head deputy's interviewing them now."

Marshall stood and held out his hand. "I'd appreciate you keeping us up to speed," he said. He shook first Bill's hand and then mine. Holding mine a mite longer than was natural, he said, "You've always been special to Laura, Milt. You were a good friend to her when she really needed one. I hope you can remain that way."

"I want to find the boy bad as y'all do," I said.

"I hope for the same reason," he said, letting go of my hand and staring deep into my eyes.

I nodded and Bill and I headed out the door, with me wanting to run to the squad car just as bad as I had at Amanda's mama's trailer. Only this time, I would be running alone and from something quite a bit different.

Emmett Hopkins called me at home that evening. "Well, talked to about forty of 'em, Milt," he said. "All spouting the party line. Trent was upset. He and Amanda left after lights-out. End of story."

"Nothing else?"

"I tried to get some background on what happened on the

days leading up to their departure, but all I got was some gobbledygook about the Source and the Light and all that shit."

"Nothing interesting?" I asked.

"Well, one interesting thing. Of all those I interviewed, about thirty-five of the forty were women, and of those thirty-five, I'd say at least fifteen of 'em were visibly pregnant."

"That is interesting."

"Ain't it just?"

"You going back over tonight to talk to the ones work in town?" I asked.

"Jasmine's gonna do it, if that's okay."

"Sure. You got her up to speed?"

"No, Sheriff, I just thought I'd let her go in there and wing it."

"Uppity and sarcastic, all in the same sentence."

"I'm a Renaissance man."

"That you are. See you tomorrow."

"Think we gonna have to call off the game-watching?"

"And he said he was smart."

Emmett hung up in my ear.

Jean was already in bed when I crawled in my side. She had her reading glasses perched on her nose and was reading a medical journal, yellow highlighter in hand, marking passages as she went. It's mostly nice be married to a smart woman, but sometimes it can be a pain in the ass. This was one of those times.

I had to tell her I saw Laura. There was no way around that. Normally I wouldn't disturb her while she was working in bed, but this wasn't normal. This was Laura.

I'd called home from the office earlier in the day, told her about finding the dead girl. But since I got home, Jean hadn't asked anything about how my day had gone, and I hadn't volunteered, not while Johnny Mac was up. But now he was asleep and I had my husbandly duty to do.

That's when I had my brainstorm. It happens to me sometimes—not often, but when it does I like it.

"Honey," I said, "you got a minute?"

She looked at me over the top of her reading glasses, yellow marking pen still poised over the text of her journal. She wasn't giving an inch. Not that woman.

"What?" she said.

"I know you got a lot on your plate right now," I said. My wife's the head psychiatrist at Long Branch Memorial Hospital. Actually, right now, she's the only psychiatrist at Long Branch Memorial Hospital, which is why I spoke the truth when I said she had a lot on her plate. "But I was hoping you could help me out with some research."

She didn't say anything, just studied me over the rims of her reading glasses.

"This religious retreat—the Seven Trumpets?"

She just looked at me.

"I was hoping you could get on your computer, see what you can find out about them."

Finally she spoke. "Why?"

I shrugged my shoulders. "Something ain't kosher there, that's for sure."

She put down the yellow marker and took off her reading glasses. I wasn't sure whether this was a good sign or a sign that I should be very, very afraid.

"Did you talk to Laura again?" she finally asked.

"Actually, Bill Williams and me drove over to her house. Met her husband. Nice guy," I said.

Jean just looked at me.

"Honey," I said, "I really need your help on this."

"You're trying to placate me," my wife said. "Or manipulate me into not worrying about Laura. That's not going to work, Milt."

I sighed. Well, it had seemed like a good idea at the time. I was pretty sure we were gonna have a discussion, and as any man can tell you, having a discussion with your wife is never about baseball, the weather, or yard work. Having a discussion with your wife meant "relationship." And when your wife's a psychiatrist, that can get pretty damned hairy, let me tell you.

"I'm not trying to do any of that," I said, knowing when I said that, we both knew it was a lie.

"I get the impression from you that you feel that I should feel threatened by that woman's return to your life," Jean said. Just right out there. That's the way she does things. No hiding, no beating around the bush. Just *boom*. There it is. I've always thought bushes needed a little beating, personally.

"She's not back in my life, honey. This is business. I'm a cop. She's got a problem. It's business. Nothing I can do about it."

She stared at me. "That's not what I said," she said.

"You want me to hand this over to Emmett?" I asked.

"Milt, are we discussing the same thing?"

"You said you felt threatened—"

"Honey, that's not what I said," Jean said, putting the glasses on the comforter between us. "I feel that that's what you expect from me, though. Obviously I'm right about that."

I was getting confused. "What I expect? That I expect you to be threatened?"

"Don't you?"

"Ah, well, aren't you?" I asked.

Jean took a deep breath and stared off into space for a minute. Then she said, "I don't like what she did to you in the past. But that's just what it was—the past. I'm not jealous, if

41

that's what you think, honey. But I am worried."

"About what?" I asked.

"That she can suck you in again—"

"Now, Jean, honey, there's no way—"

She patted my hand and smiled at me. "I'm not talking sexually here, Milt. I know you well enough to know that I don't need to worry about that. I'm talking emotionally. That woman is a bottomless emotional pit and I don't want her dragging you down there with her."

I thought about what she said, remembering my time with Laura, and knew in my heart that Jean was right: half of what had happened between me and Laura had been my need to protect her. I guessed that might be what Jean was talking about.

"So what do I do to keep that from happening?" I asked, being as straight with her as she was with me.

"Give the case to Emmett," she said, "or someone else."

I sighed. "Honey, I can't do that! Emmett's on two cases right now as it is, Jasmine's working that prostitute thing, and you know I can't rely on Dalton to do anything more than drive a squad car."

"Hank Dobbins," she said.

"In Tulsa for another two weeks," I said.

She stared off into space again.

"Talk to me, honey," I said.

"You still have feelings for her," she said. Not a question, a statement.

"Yeah, you're right, I do. And they're mixed. Part of me remembers how I felt about her, the other part of me hates her guts. That's kinda normal, huh?"

Jean smiled. "Pretty normal," she said.

"And I wasn't really trying to placate you when I asked for your help—"

42

She gave me a look.

"Okay," I said. "Maybe I was. That doesn't mean it's not true. I do need your help. I wanna know something about this Seven Trumpets place. They're really into computers from what I've heard, so they gotta have a Web site, or something, right?"

Jean looked thoughtful for a moment. "Probably," she said.

"Can you get on the computer tomorrow and see what you can find out?"

"I could probably do that," she said.

"Meanwhile," I said, moving the reading glasses from between us, "you wanna mess around?"

When I woke up Sunday morning, I was surprised to hear Jean and Johnny Mac in the kitchen having breakfast. They usually went to an early mass together, but it was barely eight o'clock.

I got up and put on my pants and went into the kitchen. "Morning," I said, kissing Jean on the cheek and ruffling Johnny Mac's hair. "Y'all back from church already?" I asked.

Jean tossed me a ream of papers. "I've been busy," she said, smiling. "God will forgive me."

I took the papers she'd handed me. "What's this?"

"Everything I could find on the Internet on the Seven Trumpets. You want to read it or should I give you a quick summary?"

I needed to read it, but I could do that later. "Summary," I said.

Jean smiled and picked up the papers, lining them up evenly and squaring the edges.

"Well, basically, the Seven Trumpets is a mishmash of pseudo-Eastern religions, a little Judaism, some Christianity, and a whole lot of *Star Trek*."

"*Star Trek?*" I asked, scalding my tongue on the coffee.

"Remember the Heaven's Gate group in San Diego? They thought the mother ship was coming to get them and they all committed suicide?"

"Oh, yeah, I remember that," I said.

"This one doesn't seem to think the mother ship is coming. As far as I can tell, they think the world is going to end and only they will survive. The Seven Trumpets," she said, pointing at a yellow-highlighted line and quoting, " 'will replenish the earth.' "

"Fifteen pregnant women," I said.

"What?" Jean asked.

I looked up from the printout. "Emmett said he saw at least fifteen pregnant women when he was interviewing the residents yesterday. And most of the residents were women—like three-quarters of 'em."

Jean nodded. "That makes sense. If you're going to replenish the earth, you need more cows than bulls."

I shuddered. "That's disgusting," I said. I got up and went to the phone, picking it up and dialing my office. Jasmine picked up on the first ring.

"It's Milt," I said.

"Hi, Milt," she said, sounding for all the world like the thought of talking to me was the saddest thing she'd ever heard of.

"You interview those people at the retreat last night? The ones who work in town?"

"Yes, sir," she said.

"Got one quick question for you: How many of 'em were women and how many of 'em were pregnant?"

"That's two questions, Milt," Jasmine said.

"Jasmine, honey, that was almost a joke, and I'm real proud of you, but now's not the time."

"Well, all of 'em were women, Milt. And, well, now that

you mention it, I think there were a few pregnant ones. But I'm not sure how many."

"You got your report written up?"

"I'm working on it," she said.

"Include that information and fax it to me ASAP."

I got off the phone and thought about it all for a minute. Whatever any of it had to do with the death of Amanda Nederwald was, at this point, lost on me.

"What did she say?" Jean asked as I came back to the table.

"All women and some of 'em, she wasn't sure how many, looked pregnant."

Jean chuckled. "Boy, would I like to get my hands on your Brother Grigsby. I'd make it in the *New England Journal* for sure."

"I need to go out there again tomorrow," I said. I grinned at her. "Wanna go with me?"

"What time?" she asked.

I shrugged my shoulders. "Your call."

Her weekly planner was never far from her side. Now it resided on the table next to her. She flipped it open to Monday. "I've got a ten-o'clock and a lunch meeting with the board. Then my afternoon's full. How early in the morning can we get out there?"

"Oh, the earlier the better," I said.

4

I lay in bed that night, my own reading glasses perched on my own nose. The printout Jean had made on the Seven Trumpets was in my hand and it made for some interesting reading.

Welcome to the homepage of the Seven Trumpets, a communal Family of True Believers of God and His Emissary here on earth, our Source of Light who will speak on these pages. Through Him, our Source, God has touched us and taught us His teachings for here on earth, as it will be in Heaven.

In these pages our Source will tell of God's gift of our Name, the Seven Trumpets, and how this Name has truer meaning than those of any manmade church or religion here on earth.

Our Name is two thousand years in the making and comes to us from God through his Emissary, our Source, who came to us through God's Divine Intervention, traveling through Time and Dimension to reach us here on earth and bring us the message and our Name.

Oh, boy, I thought. Here comes the *Star Trek* stuff. So, looks to me like what they were saying was good old Brother Grigsby was not of this world, just as Barry had said. And, as Emmett had asked, the answer appeared to be, "Yep, he's an alien."

I read on:

Now hear the words of God, as brought to us by our own Source and Light:

In the Book of Revelation, God spoke through the apostle John, telling us of what was to come. And in so doing, we were brought our name:

When the Lamb of God broke the Seventh Seal, there was silence throughout Heaven. Then the seven angels who stand before God were given seven trumpets:

The first angel blew his trumpet and hail and fire, mixed with blood, were thrown down upon the earth.

The second angel blew his trumpet, and a great mountain of fire was thrown into the sea.

The third angel blew his trumpet and a great flaming star fell out of the sky, burning like a torch.

The fourth angel blew his trumpet and a third of the sun was struck, and a third of the moon, and a third of the stars, and they became dark.

The fifth angel blew his trumpet and a star fell to the earth from the sky and the angel was given the key to the shaft of the bottomless pit.

The sixth angel blew his trumpet and a voice was heard speaking from the four horns of the gold altar that stands in the presence of God.

The seventh angel blew his trumpet and there were loud voices shouting in Heaven, "The whole world has now become the Kingdom of our Lord and of his Christ, and He will reign forever and ever."

Okay, I thought, that I recognized from Sunday school. So what's the point?

The source—excuse me, Brother Grigsby—went on:

It is through our God the true Father that we were given our name, The Seven Trumpets, to always remember and rejoice in the fact that the earth will soon become the Kingdom where we will reign in his name.

We are one with God and the Universe and know that we will be joining the Next Level in this life.

Join us in aspiring to the Next Level here on earth. We need not journey to our other home outside this realm to truly know the Kingdom of God. We need only Believe. Belief is the universal truth. Join us on our journey.

For those of you not in our area who will be unable to attend our services in the flesh, please join us online, every Monday night, 8 P.M. central time.

The Message from our Source is clear: the Way to truth is through the Light and the Light is our Source.

That was just the first page—the commercial.
The second page was a little more interesting.

We are the ones coming out of the great tribulation. We washed our robes in the blood of the Lamb and made them white. That is why we are standing in front of the throne of God, serving him day and night in His Temple. And I, who sit on the throne next to our living God will live among you and shelter you. You will never again be hungry or thirsty, and you will be fully protected from the scorching noontime heat. For

48

the Lamb who stands in front of the throne will be your Shepherd. I will lead you to the springs of life-giving water. And I, as God's Emissary, will wipe away all your tears.

Oh, boy, I thought. Now Brother Grigsby had decided he was Christ.

"Jean," I said, breaking her away from her medical journal.

"Hum?"

"Did you read this here?" I asked.

"Oh, yeah," she said.

"Did you notice anything funny about the pronouns?" I asked.

"You mean the 'we' in the beginning changing to 'you' as the 'I' took over for God?"

"Yep, that's what I meant. What does it mean?"

Jean took the page out of my hands and reread it. "Well, off the top of my head, without having met your Brother Grigsby, I'd say at some point he moved from being one of his own flock to being Christlike in his own mind. It seems to me he thinks he's a prophet, somewhat like Jesus."

"Maybe that's why he chose Prophesy County as his base," I said.

Jean laughed. "Good point. I wouldn't be at all surprised."

I kissed her, our reading glasses clicking together. "You really wanna read that journal?" I asked, slipping my hand under the covers. The first things to go were our glasses.

The next morning we dropped Johnny Mac off early at the baby-sitter's and hightailed it up to the Seven Trumpets. The barbs were in place at the cattle guard and the gate was padlocked. Using my cell phone, I called the compound.

"This is Sheriff Kovak," I said. "Who am I speaking to?"

"Hey, Milt, it's Barry."

49

"Hey, Barry. I'm down at the gate. Need to be let in."

"We had your people here all weekend, Milt. Aren't y'all about through?"

"We don't know who did it yet, Barry, so no, we ain't through."

"Monday morning is a time of spiritual—"

"Come open the gate, Barry, or I'll go get a court order. Which is gonna piss me off, and you don't want to piss me off, Barry."

"God, Milt, you're a pain in the ass. Be right there."

He hung up in my ear.

It was a little after seven when we saw the bicycle tooling down the road. Barry glared at me, then took off the padlock, did the thing with the barbs, and held the gates open for us to enter. I pulled through and stopped, waiting for him to close up.

He pointed at his bike and then the Jeep, and I nodded my head. Barry opened the back and tossed the bike in, then got in back behind Jean.

"This here is Dr. McDonnell," I said, by way of introducing Jean. "She's here to observe. Dr. McDonnell, this is Barry Leventhwart—"

"Brother Barry, Doctor. I have no need for humanist names. May I ask what kind of doctor you are?"

Jean turned around in her seat to look at him. "Psychiatrist," she said.

Barry grinned. " 'Cause we're all nuts, huh, Milt?"

"You said it, Barry," I said, "not me."

"So are you the psychiatrist that married my Aunt La-Donna's ex-husband?" Barry asked, the grin still in place.

Jean looked at me. In all the excitement I'd forgotten to mention the connection to yet another woman from my past.

The silence was excruciating. So I broke it. "Yeah, she's my wife," I said.

Nobody had an answer for that.

The place looked the same as I pulled the Jeep up next to the pavilion, except for the old school bus parked nearby.

In answer to my query, Barry said, "I drive that into town for the people who work off the compound."

The place was deserted, but I could hear hammering and other sounds of construction, and farm machines out in the fields, plowing and doing what they do. I've spent most of my life trying not to find out what farm equipment does. If I don't know, I figure nobody will ever ask me to help 'em.

"Brother Grigsby is having his morning service, Milt. It's private. Wait here and you can see—Milt, I mean it, don't go in there! Milt!"

But I already had the doors open.

There was a bunch of 'em, all right. Must have been close to a hundred, sitting on the little hard benches, standing and leaning against the walls. Brother Grigsby was up at the pulpit and he was on fire.

"I saw a woman clothed with the sun, with the moon beneath her feet, and a crown of twelve stars on her head. She was pregnant, and she cried out in the pain of labor as she awaited her delivery."

Women jumped to their feet, lots of them with bellies so swollen they looked about to pop, screaming hallelujahs and amens at the tops of their lungs.

"But the Bible doesn't say it all, my sisters! The Bible calls women unclean! Is that true?"

The few men there joined with the women in screaming, "No!"

"Woman is purity itself! Beauty and joy! Blessed be the women!"

51

People turned to one another, kissing swollen bellies while mothers-to-be beamed. Funny, I didn't see any children. Hadn't seen any children on my previous visit either.

"You will bring us to the Highest Level! You will populate our new home with your seeds! With our seeds! We have planted, and we will reap what we have sown!"

The noise was deafening. And the service went on in that vein. Jean and I left the sanctuary, followed closely on our heels by Brother Barry.

"Now, Milt," Barry whined, sounding a lot as he had at ten when he didn't get his way. "Y'all aren't allowed in there! I told you that!"

"Any word on Trent?" I asked him.

He shook his head. "Nobody knows anything, Milt. We've told your people that. It's time y'all went on and left us alone."

The doors of the main building opened and people came out, some clapping, most still singing. There were a hell of a lot of pregnant women in the group, and I figured that some of the ones who didn't look pregnant might be in the early stages. The women outnumbered the men at least four to one.

Brother Grigsby was the last out the door, his arms around two very pregnant women, a smile on his face as he looked down into the faces of the two.

He saw us and removed his arms, pushing the two women lightly away. He walked up to us, extending his hand to me. "Sheriff, I thought I saw you at the back of the sanctuary. It's a pleasure to see you again." He looked at Jean, and boy, did I not like the way he looked at Jean. "And you are?"

Jean was dressed for work in a spring-looking floral dress. She leaned on her crutches, her braces getting dusty from the dirt of the compound.

"Jean McDonnell," she said. "Milt's wife."

He took her hand, smiling big. "How wonderful!" He

leaned forward and whispered something in Jean's ear. She pulled away and moved next to me.

Brother Grigsby turned to me. "And what brings you out here at such an early hour, Sheriff?"

"I wanted to have a talk with you, Grigsby."

"Certainly." He extended his arm, pointing toward the chairs and tables under the pavilion. "Why don't we sit down? Brother Barry, please have Sister Ruth bring us refreshment." To us, he said, "We don't imbibe spirits here, Sheriff, which include coffee, tea, and chocolate. But we do have some wonderful juices."

"That's fine," I said.

"There are a lot of teas that don't have caffeine," Jean said.

Brother Grigsby smiled. "You mean like chamomile, ginseng, et cetera?"

Jean nodded.

"True, but they do contain earthly drugs, Doctor." He cocked his head at the look on Jean's face. "Of course I know who you are, Dr. McDonnell. There is no way I would move into a community without knowing who my potential adversaries might be."

Jean raised an eyebrow. I love it when she does that. "Adversaries?" she asked.

"Are you a member of the AMA?" he asked.

Jean smiled. "Yes," she said.

"Then you are part of the conspiracy," Grigsby said.

"Which conspiracy is that?" Jean asked.

"The medical community, the legal community, so-called organized religion—they all believe that a religion not of their own making is a 'cult,' and that anyone who would belong to such an organization has to be crazy, and therefore it's okay to kidnap them from their true family."

"Have you had a lot of that?" Jean asked.

"We have been blessed here," Grigsby said. "You people haven't bothered us much."

"I'm not 'you people,' Mr. Grigsby, and you have no idea how I operate."

God, I love it when my wife gets that voice going—especially when it's not aimed at me.

The young pregnant woman I'd seen on my first visit—identified as Barry's wife—came out of the building, carrying a tray loaded with drinks. I started to jump up to help her, but Grigsby held my arm. "Sister Ruth is as strong as any man," he said, his hand going to her hip as she laid the tray down. He smiled up at her. "Isn't that so, Sister Ruth?"

The look the young woman gave Grigsby was one I wouldn't want my wife giving another man. To me she said, "I'm on a higher level, Sheriff. It gives me the strength to serve our Source."

Sister Alma, Grigsby's wife, had come out of the building and was standing close by, watching. She smiled as Sister Ruth came by her, and gave her arm a squeeze.

Oh, yeah, these were a strange bunch all right.

"I need to ask you a few questions, Grigsby," I said.

Grigsby spread his arms wide. "Anything, Sheriff. My only aim is to cooperate with you to find out what happened to our poor little Sister Amanda."

"Well, that's great, Grigsby. First, what made those two kids decide to stay here after the weekend was over?"

"You'd have to ask them that," he said.

"That's gonna be difficult," I said, "what with one dead and one missing. Surely they talked to you about staying."

"Brother Trent spoke to Brother Barry, I believe."

"And Barry's got the authority to let just anybody stay here?"

He stiffened at that and I knew I had him. Grigsby wasn't

about to admit that anybody had as much or more authority than he did.

"Brother Barry came to me, said that two of the young people who had come for the weekend wanted to join us on a permanent basis. I spoke with the two, individually, of course, to make sure they were pure of heart and understood our true purpose—"

"Which is?" I asked.

"Which is what, Sheriff?" Grigsby asked, no longer smiling.

"Your true purpose. What exactly is that?"

"To worship God in our way, of course," he said, the smile back. "And to reach a higher level with his guidance."

"Uh-huh," I said. "And did they understand?"

"Sister Amanda did," he said, smiling. "Such a sweet child. Truly ready for the next level."

"And Trent?"

He shrugged. "At first I thought he understood, I thought he was eager to begin his journey. But by the end of the weekend I wasn't so sure."

"Why's that?"

He shrugged again. "Because he began to complain. He wanted Amanda to leave and she didn't want to. He had no right trying to thrust his will upon her."

"As opposed to you making her decision for her?" I said.

Grigsby stood up. "I'm feeling a great deal of doubt from you, Sheriff. Negative energy comes off you like skin off a snake. I must ask you to leave."

He turned and headed back into the main building.

"I got a few more questions, Grigsby—" I started, but I felt a hand on my arm.

Turning, I saw Barry. "You must leave, Milt," he said, and there was fear in his voice and his eyes.

"Why?" I asked.

"Because the Source has commanded it be so," he said.

"Oh, for God's sake," I said, took Jean by the arm, and led her back to the Jeep. The Source was becoming a pain in the ass.

On our way back to town, I asked Jean what Grigsby had said to her when he whispered in her ear.

"Oh, that," she said, laughing slightly. "Good news, honey. Our dear Brother Grigsby said he can heal me."

"What?" I said, almost running the Jeep off the road.

"Yep. That's what he whispered in my ear. 'I can make you whole again.' "

"That son of a bitch—"

Jean patted my hand. "That man is something else, Milt. I've never seen an ego like that. I was kidding last night when I said I could do a paper on him, but my God—"

"You're not getting near that freak again!" I said, madder than I'd been in a long time.

"You wanted me to observe him, Milt. And I did. Do you want my input?"

"No, I just want him dead."

"Milt, you're overreacting."

"Goddamn right I'm overreacting. I'm going to overreact all over his ass!"

"I'm a trained observer, Milt. I would think you'd want my opinions."

I sighed. "Of course I want your opinions. I just can't believe that son of a bitch said that to you!"

"Honey, I've heard worse—"

"What? From who?"

"Milt!"

I sighed again. "Okay, all right. Tell me."

"As I said, Grigsby has an incredibly inflated ego, and definite delusions of grandeur, although he appears to be making those delusions a reality with the people he's gathered around him. They do more than stroke the ego, Milt."

"What makes a normal person fall for Grigsby's kind of crap?" I asked.

"Well, the first answer is, 'What's normal?' But if we can agree that there is no such thing as 'normal,' I can go on."

"Of course there's such a thing as normal—"

Jean gave me that condescending smile she gives me whenever I venture into her territory.

"Okay, fine," I said, "there's no such thing as normal."

"People who are susceptible to cults are usually loners, people not raised in any religion—or raised in a very strict religion, sometimes. Quite often people with mental illnesses are prayed upon—depressives, bipolars, schizophrenics. I think I can safely say that a great majority of these women at the retreat were raised without fathers in the home."

"So they all look at Grigsby like a father?"

"In an incestuous kind of way."

"Huh?"

"He's sleeping with all of them, Milt."

I almost lost control of the car again. "Say what?"

"I'd bet the farm that that seed being thrown around out there all belongs to our dear Brother Grigsby."

I dropped Jean off at the hospital and drove to the sheriff's department. Gladys was on the phone when I walked in the door and began waving a "while you were out" slip in my face. I took it from her. "Call your sister immediately," it said.

The last thing I wanted to do was talk to my sister Jewel Anne. We get along pretty much okay, but lately she's been having trouble with her daughter, Marlene, and seems to think I'm the answer to all her problems. I keep telling her she's talking to the wrong member of our team—she should be talking to Jean. Troubled teenagers were more her speed than mine.

But I went into my office and sat down at my desk, picking up the phone. I dialed the number.

"Milt? Is that you?" my sister said.

"You know, an hour ago I woulda said normal people answer the phone with hello, but then I found out there aren't any normal people."

"What?" she demanded.

"You rang?" I asked, sighing.

"You have to do something with Marlene!"

"She's your kid, Jewel. I got a good ten, twelve years before I have to start worrying about that."

"She's your niece! You used to care about her!"

Christ, I thought, that girl could throw guilt like nobody's business. "What's up?" I asked, knowing there was nothing I could do but just take it.

"She's back-talking me like you wouldn't believe! You should hear the things she says to me! If I so much as whispered such a thing in Mama's house—"

"Different times, Jewel. Different kids. Ground her."

"I do! If I actually followed through on all the times I've grounded her, she'd never get out of her room!"

I wasn't about to say anything about doing what you say you're going to do with a kid, consistency, and all those things Jean says are the cardinal rules of child-rearing. Since Jewel had been doing it a lot longer than Jean and me, with mixed results, I figured discretion was the better part of valor. Instead, I asked, "What do you want me to do?"

"Come over here tonight. You and Jean and John come for dinner. Then you can take her aside and talk to her."

"Jewel, she's not gonna listen to me—"

"If you assert your authority she'll listen! My God, what's the good of having a brother who's sheriff if you can't ever help me?"

I didn't dare mention the many times my being in law enforcement had come in handy for her. Didn't seem the time or place. I sighed. When Jewel had a bee in her bonnet, there wasn't much to do except give her her way. "Let me talk to Jean. Make sure she hasn't made plans—"

"I already did! She said it would be fine."

I just love it when those two gang up on me behind my back. "Okay, okay," I said. "We'll be there about six."

"I'm fixing seared tuna," she said.

I hung up, wondering if I'd have time to slip by McDonald's before we got there.

5

My sister's got three kids from her first marriage: Leonard, now off to Norman at the University of Oklahoma (he wants to be an accountant like his father, the late Henry Hotchkiss); Marlene, seventeen and a handful; and Carl, the baby at fourteen. My sister and I weren't close growing up as there was a thirteen-year difference in our ages, but when I got a call a few years ago, telling me my sister's husband Henry had been killed and that Jewel had been shot, too, and was lying in a coma in a Houston hospital, I hightailed it down there to take care of the kids and see what I could do. The police just figured it was one of those murder/suicide things husbands and wives tend to do. With Jewel being the shooter.

It helped our relationship a little bit that I was able to find out who killed her husband and why.

After that she and her kids moved back to Prophesy County to live with me. That's a time I don't like to think about too much. That girl can surely ride roughshod over just about anybody, and, believe you me, I was no match for her.

It wasn't long, though, before her high school boyfriend showed up. Harmon Monk was a married man, but it didn't take long for his wife and two daughters to take off for Oklahoma City and leave Harmon what you might call "available." Harmon and Jewel were married before the ink was dry on his divorce papers.

Which is kind of ironic, when you think about it. My daddy made Jewel Anne break up with Harmon back in high school because he was the no-good son of a pig farmer and didn't— and Daddy was sure wouldn't—have a pot to piss in. But ol' Harmon fooled everybody. After his daddy died, Harmon took his part of his daddy's pig farm and turned it into a car graveyard, where he started selling parts. By the time Jewel moved back to Prophesy County, Harmon owned the biggest chain of auto-parts stores in our end of the state.

And now Jewel lived in a great big, Tara-looking semi-mansion that she'd been redecorating for the past three years.

I pulled the Jeep into the circular drive and stopped in front of the Tara-looking front door.

Jewel opened the door, a pained expression on her face. "If you don't talk to her right this minute, I might just shoot her!"

I sighed. "Where is she?"

"Where do you think? In her room with the door closed! And locked, as far as I can tell."

Jean leaned forward and the two hugged. "She's just in her rebellious stage, Jewel. . . ."

Breaking apart, Jewel said, "Yeah, well, she may not live through it! Milton! Do something!"

I saw my brother-in-law Harmon sitting in the living room. He had the evening paper in front of his face, but was peeking out at me around it. Chickenshit, I thought.

I sighed and headed up the curving stairway to the second floor. The thick rug squished under my feet as I made my way down the hall to Marlene's room. I knocked on the door, but there was no answer.

61

I said, "Marlene, it's me. Uncle Milt. Let me in."

I heard a sob, feet lightly pounding across the carpet, then the sound of a bolt turning. She let me in, then slammed the door behind me, throwing the lock.

I looked around the room. Hell, if I'd had this room when I was a teenager, I'd want to stay in it all the time, too.

There was a queen-sized bed with canopy, all done in cheery shades of green with matching curtains on the windows, and pillows and stuffed animals crowded together on the bed. Across the room from her bed was an entertainment center filled with stereo, TV, DVD player, and all the other playthings of your modern American well-off teenager. Next to the large windows was a desk with a state-of-the-art computer.

Marlene threw herself into my arms and began wailing. "Oh, Uncle Milt!" she cried. "Look what she's *done* to me!"

I got out my handkerchief and handed it to her, pushing her back a little so I could see her face. "You wanna tell me what's going on, little girl?"

"It's *her*! She *hates* me!"

"She doesn't hate—"

She threw herself dramatically away from me and landed sprawled face-first on the bed.

"She does! She *hates* me! She wants me to *die*!"

"Your mama loves you more—"

She sat up and looked at me. "You're on *her* side! I should have *known*!"

"You wanna tell me what set this off?" I asked.

"I wouldn't tell you the time of *day*! You'd just go tell *her*!"

"Well, if she needs to know the time of day—" I broke off seeing the look on my niece's face. She wasn't in the mood for funny. "Marlene, is there something going on you need to talk about?"

Her whole body shuddered as she took in a deep breath. "She's always on me! Always!"

"Tell me how," I said, patting her arm by way of encouragement.

In a high falsetto, Marlene mimicked, "Where are you going? Who are you going with? When will you be back? What did you make on that paper? When's that test? Who's that boy who called? Are you seeing him? Who's his family?"

Well, personally I didn't think most of those questions were all that awful, me being a grown-up and a daddy and everything, but I figured now wasn't the time to say so. Instead I said, "You know what I think? I think you and your mama need to sit down with Aunt Jean and work out some rules, ya know?"

"Rules? Rules! All I've got around her are *rules*!"

"I mean for both of you. Rules for your mama too—"

"Like *she'd* go for that!"

"Honey, it's worth a try."

Marlene sobbed again. "She's so fuckin'—"

Automatically I said, "Watch your language—"

Which just set her off again. "I don't even have the *right to talk*! Not even with *you*! Even *you* hate me!"

"Oh, for God's sake, Marlene—"

She threw herself across the bed again, bursting into sobs. I got up and left the room.

Once downstairs, we all sat down in the fancy dining room, prepared to eat my sister's seared tuna. I like my beef rare, but that's about the only thing. The raw tuna sitting on my plate looked decidedly like bait to me.

Luckily my niece's behavior kept Jewel from noticing that the little bit of tuna I'd put on my plate I was sneaking onto Johnny Mac's. Not that he'd eat it either, but she'd forgive him the oversight.

"What did she say?" Jewel asked.

"That you hate her," I said, sawing on a piece of under-cooked potato with my knife.

Jewel's face swelled with unshed tears. "I don't hate her! Why would she think I hate her?"

Jean reached out across the table to take Jewel's hand. "Maybe I should have a talk with her, Jewel."

Jewel smiled a weak, sad smile, tears glinting in her eyes. "Somebody's got to. I can't take much more! Neither can Harmon."

Harmon, who sat at the head of the table, refrained from saying anything.

Jean got up from the table. "Let me go talk to her," she said, and I knew this was just her sneaky way of getting out of eating the tuna.

She left the room, taking her crutches to help her up the long climb of the stairs.

"I just don't know what to do, Milt," Jewel said. "She brings the strangest people into this house! I don't know where she finds the kids she's hanging out with. They're just not normal."

Carl, the fourteen-year-old, made a strangled sound at the end of the table. "Oh, have you got two cents' worth you want to share with us, young man?" Jewel demanded.

He made another sound, in the negative, I think, and sat there pushing his food around on his plate.

"She'd be on the phone all night long if I'd let her—"

"Milt, could you come up here a minute?" Jean called from the stairs.

Jewel threw her napkin into her plate. "Why do I even bother trying to make a good meal for you people?" She jumped up and ran into the kitchen.

I headed for the stairs. Jean was standing at the landing. "You need to come into Marlene's room," she said.

I followed her in. The room was empty, and by that, I mean Marlene wasn't in it. "Where is she?" I asked, going to her bathroom to look—which was also empty.

Jean pointed to the windowsill. The window was open, the screen gone. And on the sill were drops of bright red blood.

My sister Jewel was a blithering idiot. I mean, more than usual. Harmon had his arm around her as we all stared into the empty, slightly blood-smeared room. On seeing the blood, Carl, the youngest, said, "Cool!"

At his words, Jewel gasped and fell against Harmon, bursting into tears.

"It's not his fault, Jewel," I said. "Bad choice of words," I said, looking at Carl, who nodded.

"Sorry, Mom," he said, his voice a lot deeper than the last time I'd heard it. But, then again, he didn't speak much and I'm not sure when was the last time I'd actually heard his voice.

Jewel threw her arms around Carl. "It's not your fault, swee-tie. I'm sorry."

Carl patted his mother's back, his head, I noticed for the first time, a couple of inches higher than hers. "I know, Mom, I know."

Jewel Anne pulled herself away from her son and turned on me. "Well? Why aren't you *doing* something?" she demanded.

"Y'all stay here. Carl, watch the women. Harmon, come with me." Having *done* something, I went downstairs and out the front door, Harmon following me, and we went around to the side of the house, under the opened window of Marlene's room.

There was an indention in the dirt of the flower bed, not so much a footprint as a slight hole, but I noticed a drop of blood on the white petal of a gardenia.

"Oh, Lord," Harmon said.

We both looked around the lavish grounds, then headed toward the wooded area at the back of Harmon's seven acres. We didn't see any more blood. We also didn't see footprints or chewing-gum wrappers, or cigarette butts. None of the clues I'd been hoping for.

"Tell me the truth, Harmon," I said. "You think she ran away?"

Harmon shrugged. "Lord, Milt, I don't know. She coulda. She's been mad enough. But the blood—"

"Yeah, I know. The blood."

I got back to the house and called it in, getting all the deputies from the sheriff's department, and then called the Bishop police force out. Both of 'em.

"It don't look good, Milt," said Maypearl Leslie, chief of police of Bishop. Maypearl was a big ol' gal who liked blood-red lipstick and fuchsia nail polish. Bishop hadn't had policing other than the sheriff's department up until two years ago, when there was a string of burglaries the town folk didn't think I and my deputies solved fast enough. Since the combined income of the town folk of Bishop is a little less than the national debt, they decided to go ahead and hire their own. And they did.

Maypearl had been with the Texas Highway Patrol and took the job in a heartbeat. She brought along her little sister, June Rose, then just out of the academy, as her backup. June Rose is another big ol' gal, who shunned most girly affectations, except for the large pink rose tattooed on the inside of her left arm, and between the two of them they did tend to keep a peaceable community. I can't say I've ever had a bit of trouble with either of them.

"I know it," I said, a bit irritated at being reminded of the obvious.

66

"The mama getting that list of friends I asked for?" Maypearl inquired.

"I already had her working on that, Maypearl, me being an officer of the law and all." Okay, I was really getting irritated, but then I felt I was due.

"I'm only thinking I should take over here, Milt, what with you being personally involved and all," Maypearl said.

"Take over?"

"It's my jurisdiction, Milt," Maypearl said.

"I beg to differ. Harmon's house is not in the city limits of Bishop. It's in the county."

"You didn't read about our newest annexation? Took over this whole road up to Derry Creek."

Which put Harmon's house smack-dab in Bishop township. I'd read it but forgot.

I sighed. "Okay, fine, Maypearl. You're in charge. But I'd be grateful if you'd let me help."

She smiled, showing some healthy gums and expensive bridgework. Must have gotten that while she was still with the Highway Patrol and had dental insurance, I figured. "How about that list of friends?" she said.

I sighed again. "I'll go get it."

I went in the house. Jewel and Jean were in the living room, Jean writing down names and numbers Jewel was reading from her address book. Jewel's eyes were red-rimmed and she hic-cuped when she talked. On seeing me, she said, "Where's Harmon?"

"Out helping the police," I said.

"And Carl?"

"The same," I said.

She nodded. "I'm the worst mother in the world," she said, and began to sob.

Jean put down her paper and moved to the couch next to

Jewel, taking her in her arms and murmuring soothingly to her. I looked around and found Johnny Mac on the floor in front of the fireplace, his toy dinosaurs spread about in front of him, seemingly having a grand ol' time.

I picked up the pad of paper Jean had been writing on and tore off the top sheet. "I'll just get them started on this. Y'all finish up when you can," I said, then slithered out of the room.

June Rose was up in Marlene's bedroom with Jasmine Bodine, taking samples of the blood to send to the lab in Tulsa and fingerprinting the windowsill and anything else that looked helpful. I went outside to where Maypearl was interviewing Harmon.

"Anyplace you could think of she'd go if she was in trouble?" Maypearl asked.

Harmon shook his head. "She likes to go to the movies in town, and to that video-game place on Main Street. And to church. That's about it. And school, of course."

"You think she'd run off to school? Or church?"

Harmon shook his head. "Probably not."

Carl cleared his throat. "She's been meeting with Clifford Shaunsee over at the Derry Creek Bridge."

We all looked at Carl. Finally I said, "Thank you, Carl."

"Yes, sir," he said. "Want me to show you where?"

"That'd be real helpful, son."

"Why don't you and the boy handle that, Milt?" Maypearl said.

I stifled a salute and then thought maybe I'd let being in charge at the sheriff's department go to my head a little, and packed Carl in the Jeep for the short drive to the Derry Creek bridge.

It was dark as pitch out, no moon shining, and the starlight sure wasn't filtering down beneath the trees around the Derry Creek Bridge. I left the headlights on on the Jeep, knowing that was the biggest flashlight I had, then took one flashlight out of the glove compartment and one out from under the driver's seat, handing the smaller one to Carl.

It was quiet as the grave, our feet making crunching noises on the loose gravel of the paved road. The shoulder was wet from a recent rain, and we moved onto it, going toward the bank leading down to the creek and under the bridge.

It wasn't really all that quiet—I could hear crickets and katydids, the slight rush of the rain-swollen creek, and a frog up the creek a bit, singing its night song. We shone our lights under the bridge, finding only empty beer cans and used condoms—something I didn't want to think about or mention to my sister. We walked under the bridge, heading upcreek.

We walked for about a quarter mile, shining our lights on both sides of the creek, finding nothing. At a narrow point in the creek, I followed Carl's lead and we used rocks in the water as stepping stones to cross to the other bank, then headed back the way we'd come. Under the bridge on this side of the creek it was a lot cleaner than where we'd been, but still empty of life.

We went downcreek a ways, then Carl jumped the creek to the other side. I splashed across, getting my brand-new Nikes all wet. We went back to the Jeep, started it up, and kept on the road, crossing the bridge and going slowly down the dark road, my flashlight in my hand, shining it on the side of the road, hoping to find her, hoping not.

"What do you think, Carl?" I finally asked.

He shook his head. "I dunno. She's crazy."

"Yeah," I said, letting the unspoken hang between us.

"I think I want to go home and call Leonard," he said.

Most of Jewel's troubles with Marlene had started the previous fall, when Leonard had gone off to college. Leonard had been the touchstone for these kids, the thing that had kept them together when their father was murdered and their mother lay in a Houston hospital in a coma. When they came to live with me, I had noticed the two younger ones listened to Leonard more than they did to either of the adults in the house—me and Jewel Anne. But Leonard had handled it in such a way that his mother had rarely seen it. Now she was paying for that oversight.

I headed back to the house. It would be up to Jewel whether or not Leonard was called in, not that I could see where he could do anything I and the rest of law enforcement couldn't.

Jewel Anne was totally against the idea of calling Leonard. "I don't want to worry him," she said. "He's got finals in a week." She wrapped her arms round her chest. "If . . . if anything . . . bad happens, that will be soon enough to call him."

Carl straightened up to his full height, which I was beginning to notice was getting close to mine—and him only fourteen. "I'd feel better if Leonard was here," Carl said.

"Well, I'd feel better if Marlene was here," Jewel said. "I just don't want to worry Leonard—" she started, and began to bawl again.

"Jewel," Harmon said, "calm down, honey. Carl's feeling just as bad as the rest of us, right?" he said, trying to pacify everybody in sight, as usual, and failing miserably, as usual.

"You know, Harmon," Carl said, "if I need you to come to my defense anytime, I'll be sure and let you know."

"Carl!" Jewel wailed.

I headed out the front door.

Maypearl was in her squad car, one leg on the ground, the other inside, the mike of her radio in her hand.

"Hey, Milt," she said as I approached. "I didn't find that Shaunsee kid on the list of names your sister gave us, so I thought I'd look him up on the computer. He's not in Bishop proper, but outside in the county."

"Oh," I said, pointing at my chest like a spoiled child, "*my* jurisdiction."

Maypearl grinned. "That's right. You wanna come with me while we go interview the little turd?"

"Sure," I said, deciding it was time to play grown-up, and got in the shotgun side of the squad car.

Maypearl squealed the tires on the circular drive as she headed out, and I wished I'd thought to suggest we go in my Jeep.

6

The Shaunsee house was in a defunct subdivision about a mile south of Derry Creek; walking distance, if you were young and in love, to my sister's house.

I could remember when the subdivision was going up, there was a lot of hope for the place. Lots of people bought half-acre lots with the promise of roads, schools, and a country club with three swimming pools and a golf course. A lot of lots were sold and about ten houses built before the developers took off for greener pastures. All that's left to remember the dream of golf course and swimming pools is a little shack at the entrance, now crumbling away, the sign saying GREEN PASTURES hanging loose and swaying in the breeze.

We pulled up in front of the Shaunsees', a nice-looking redwood-and-white-rock house, a couple of old trees in the yard, and a couple of young ones trying hard to compete. The house was well-lit and I could see well-tended flower beds. The house had real curb appeal, and could probably be sold in a heartbeat if it had been anywhere else but the defunct Green Pastures. Something told me the Shaunsee family would be enjoying this house for a long time to come.

Maypearl and I got out of her squad car and headed up the neatly trimmed walk to the front door. A wreath of spring flowers circled the peephole. We rang the bell and waited.

After a minute the door was opened by a man in his shirt-sleeves, tie at half-mast, and a beer in hand.

"Mr. Shaunsee?" I asked.

"Yes?" he said.

"I'm Sheriff Milt Kovak, Prophesy County, and this is Police Chief Leslie from Bishop. We need to speak to your son, Clifford."

Shaunsee frowned. "Clifford? What about?"

A woman came up behind him. She was in her stocking feet, still clad in the remains of a business suit. Obviously both Mr. and Mrs. Shaunsee had just gotten home from work. "Daniel?" she asked her husband.

"It's the police, Becky. They're looking for Clifford."

Mrs. Shaunsee gasped and covered her mouth with her hand. "Why on earth—"

"What's this about, Sheriff?" Mr. Shaunsee demanded.

"Clifford's not in any trouble, Mr. Shaunsee," I said, smiling. "We just need to ask him about a friend of his. She's missing, might have run away, and we're just checking all her friends—"

Shaunsee motioned to his wife. "Go get him," he said.

Mrs. Shaunsee took one last long look at me and Maypearl and headed into the depths of the house.

"Y'all come on in," Shaunsee said, leading us into a well-appointed living room. The furniture looked expensive and at the same time homey—which means they cost a lot. It was also cluttered with schoolbooks, toys, newspapers, and the usual crud that accumulates in an active home full of kids.

Mrs. Shaunsee came back in, towing two children with her; one was a girl and the boy surely wasn't old enough to be Clifford.

"He's not here!" Mrs. Shaunsee said. "Tell them!" she said, shoving the boy forward.

"He got an e-mail a couple of hours ago and took off," the kid said.

"Where did he go?" I asked.

The kid shrugged.

"You know who it was emailed him?"

Again he shrugged.

"Did he take his car?" the father asked. The boy nodded.

I looked at the girl, older than the boy who'd been talking, but probably younger than Clifford. "You know anything?" I asked.

"It was probably that Marlene. She calls here all the time. She thinks she's hot stuff."

"And if I told you Marlene is missing, what would you think?" I asked the girl.

Her eyes got big and she looked at her mother. "I dunno," she said, suddenly not so full of herself.

I looked at the mother. "Was there a note, a message on the phone, anything like that?"

Mr. Shaunsee went to their phone-message machine and shook his head. "Nothing," he said.

"No note in his room," the mother said.

"What's happened with this girl?" Shaunsee asked.

"We're not sure yet," Maypearl said. "We're still investigating."

"Investigating what?" the father demanded. "What's my son got to do with this?"

"Like I said, Mr. Shaunsee, we're just trying to talk to all Marlene's friends at the moment." I handed him a card, jotting down Jewel's home phone number on the back. "I'd appreciate a call when you hear from your son. I really need to talk to him."

"Look, I don't know where he is. If that girl's in some sort of trouble, Clifford may be too," Shaunsee said, setting his beer down as if getting serious.

Mrs. Shaunsee came up to stand beside her husband, slipping her arm in his. "Has she run away, Sheriff? Is that what you think? Or are you thinking something worse?" she asked.

I looked at Maypearl. The thing was, Shaunsee was right. With the boy now missing, too, chances were they were together, and if they just ran away, that was one thing—but the blood in Marlene's room kept interjecting itself.

"We're not sure right now, ma'am," I said, "whether Marlene's run away, or whether there may be foul play."

Mrs. Shaunsee sagged against her husband, who put his arms around her, holding her up.

"Have you got people out looking?" he asked.

"Law enforcement right now, sir, but we're thinking of calling in for volunteers."

Shaunsee sat his wife down on the nearest chair. "Leela, take care of your mother. John, you come with me. We're ready, Sheriff."

"Well, sir, I appreciate your offer, but I think it would be best if y'all stayed her and manned the phone—"

"My wife can do that—"

I nodded toward his wife, whose face was in her hands as she sobbed. "Sir, I think you need to stay here."

He looked at the white face of his daughter, the trembling hands of his son, and his sobbing wife. "Yeah," he said. "Right."

We left the Shaunsee house after getting the make, model, and license number of Clifford's car, not much wiser than when we got there.

By midnight, the volunteer fire department had set up shop on the circular drive of Jewel and Harmon's home, coordinat-

75

ing their volunteers and others in the community who had
come out to search for the missing girl—and maybe boy, too.
Who knew? This wouldn't have come about for a mere run-
away, but with the blood in the bedroom, we just didn't know.
I had an APB out to the Highway Patrol, looking for Clifford
Shaunsee's red 1982 Mustang hatchback.

Around two o'clock I was back at the house, checking in
on my family. Johnny Mac had been put to bed in Carl's room
hours ago. Carl, with his mother's reluctant permission, was
out with Harmon, searching for his sister. Jewel and Jean were
in the living room, holding hands and looking grim. Used
coffee cups lined the table in front of them.

"I think I need to call Leonard," Jewel said.

"I'll do it," I volunteered, and headed for the phone. It was
early in the morning, and I didn't want to do this to the boy,
but I could just image how he'd feel if he found out all this
after the fact—if the fact was bad.

The phone rang twice before it was picked up by a sleepy
voice. "Yeah?"

"Leonard?"

"Naw. Wait. Leonard!" the kid yelled in my ear. After a
minute, he said, "Leonard's not here, man."

"Where is he?"

"Hell if I know," he said, hanging up the phone.

Two o'clock in the morning and Marlene was missing, Clifford Shaunsee was missing, and now Leonard was missing. If
you added the missing Trent Marshall to the mix, we were
sort of having an epidemic of missing teenagers.

I turned and looked at my sister, hunched into a ball on
the sofa, staring at nothing. Jean looked at me and I motioned
for her to come.

She got up and made her way to where I was. "Leonard's
not there," I said.

Jean raised an eyebrow. "What does that mean?" she asked.

I shrugged. "He's got a date?" I asked hopefully.

That's when I heard the sputter of a badly muffled car in the driveway. I went to look out the window and saw an old model red Mustang pulling into the drive.

I headed out the front door.

It took about an hour to get hold of all the teams of volunteers and call off the hunt. It didn't take nearly that long for my sister to come running out of the house.

Leonard had been driving the car. Marlene and Clifford Shaunsee were both asleep in the backseat, curled up in each other's arms. As Leonard got out of the car, Jewel got in, leaning over to the backseat, beating on Clifford and screaming at both of them. Let me tell you, that woke up the kids for sure. Leonard and I managed to get Jewel out of the car, bodily grabbing her around the waist and hauling her out. Clifford and Marlene scrambled out the other side and stood there shamefaced, holding hands. Leonard kept his arms around his mother's waist, keeping her from leaping over the hood of the car.

I looked at Jean. "Go in and call Mr. and Mrs. Shaunsee, would ya, please. Let 'em know their boy's all right."

Jean nodded and headed for the house.

"If you touched one hair on her head, I'll kill you!" Jewel declared from the protective arms of Leonard.

"Mama," he said, "calm down now."

"See?" Marlene said, looking at me. "Do you *see* what I'm dealing with here?"

"What *you're* dealing with?" Jewel demanded. "I only hope you have a daughter who's half the trouble—" She stopped, her eyes big. "Oh, God, you're pregnant."

Marlene threw up her hands. "See? Do you *see?*"

"Mama, she's not pregnant," Leonard said, the only one in the area who seemed to have any composure at the moment. "She's upset."

"Upset? *She's* upset? I'll give her something to be upset about!"

"Jewel, honey," I said, keeping my voice soft. "Let's all go inside, have some coffee. Talk about all this."

That's when the silver Lincoln that I'd noticed in the Shaunsee's driveway came screaming into Jewel's circular drive. Both Shaunsees bailed out of the car, running for their son.

I looked up and saw Jean standing on the porch, leaning on her crutches. I could tell by looking she was tiring herself way out, but I didn't know what to do about it. Suggesting she go lie down upstairs with Johnny Mac would just get me a raised eyebrow.

Mrs. Shaunsee grabbed her son and hugged him, crying. Mr. Shaunsee grabbed one of the boy's arms. "What the hell is going on, Clifford? Where have you been?"

With Marlene still clutching the boy's other arm, he looked a bit overwhelmed. I handed Jewel off to Leonard and pushed into the melee.

"Mr. and Mrs. Shaunsee. The kids are safe. That's the main thing. Now I think we all need to go inside—"

I saw Harmon's Lincoln Navigator pull into the drive. He slammed on the brakes and he and Carl jumped out of the car, Carl almost losing his balance from the great height of the front seat.

Harmon ran up to Jewel, taking her from Leonard and Carl ran up to Leonard, throwing his arms around him. "Man, am I glad to see you!" he said.

Leonard patted his little brother on the back. "I think Uncle Milt's right," Leonard said, to all and sundry. "We need to go in the house and talk about this."

Clutching Harmon, Jewel didn't say anything, just helped lead the way into the front room. I spied Maypearl Leslie and asked her if she'd handle calling everything off.

"I thank you for your help, Maypearl. But from this point on, I think it's a family matter."

She grinned. "Fine, Milt, but if one of 'em kills the other, give me a call, okay?"

I shook my head and headed for the front door.

"This is between Marlene and me," Jewel said to the room at large. "I think everybody else should just leave."

Jean stood up, leaning heavily on her crutches. "Jewel, I think you're wrong about this. It's three o'clock in the morning and we've all been up for hours. All of us have been involved in this. Everyone has a right to know what's going on. Everyone has a right to say how they feel."

"Feel?" Jewel laughed bitterly. "Personally I *feel* like screaming! Anybody care to join me?"

"Sarcasm isn't the answer here, Jewel," Jean said.

Jewel fell back against the couch. "I'm sorry," she said softly. "I'm just so upset."

"Everyone is upset, Jewel," Jean said. "You and Harmon, the Shaunsees, and the kids. This involves everyone in this room."

Jewel nodded, closing her eyes.

I stood up. "First, as an officer of the law, I gotta ask: Marlene, where did the blood come from in your room?"

"Blood?" Marlene looked blank for a moment, then her face turned red. "Oh, Lord, I didn't think about that! Y'all thought—"

"Never mind what we thought, Marlene. Where did the blood come from?"

She stared at the floor, her face turning redder. "After you left, Uncle Milt, I was clipping my toenails and I was so upset

I clipped one too close, and then I heard Clifford's car—"

"Did you call Clifford?" I asked, knowing the phone had been taken out of her room.

She clammed up. Clifford looked at her but she just crossed her arms over her chest and stared at the floor.

"She called me all upset, Sheriff. She was talking wild. I had to come get her."

"How did you call him?" Jewel asked. "I took the phone out of your room!"

"Yeah, but you left her computer, right?" Leonard asked. Jewel nodded. "She's online, right?" Again Jewel nodded. Leonard shrugged. "Easy as pie."

"Thanks bunches, Leonard," Marlene spat, "now she's gonna take that away from me, too!"

"I don't think so," Leonard said, standing up. "I think it's about time you two figured out what's going on here. It's time Marlene got her phone back, Mama, and Marlene, it's time you stopped acting like a big old baby!"

"Am not!" she yelled.

Everyone, including Clifford, just looked at her. Marlene blushed again and stared at the rug.

I went over and stood in front of Marlene. "Look at me," I said. When she didn't, I reached down and lifted her chin up. "I want you to look at me, honey, 'cause I got something I need to tell you. Are you looking?"

"Yes," she said.

"Are you listening?"

"*Yes!*" she said.

"Good. The other day I got a call from a mother whose son was missing. Him and his girlfriend took off together. Well, guess what?" She didn't guess, so I went on. "We found the girlfriend. Naked and dead. We still ain't found the boy, and I'm afraid when we do, he's gonna be dead, too. Now, you think you can understand what you just put your mama through? What you put me and Aunt Jean through? And the Shaunsees? And Harmon? And Carl and Leonard? And about fifty people been out searching for you for hours? Giving up their sleep on a work night so they could try to find your dead little body? Any of this sinking in, girl?"

Marlene burst into tears.

I lifted her chin up again. Her eyes were squinched shut. "Open your eyes, Marlene," I said. She opened them, tears leaking out and running down her cheeks. "I'm not saying your mama isn't somewhat to blame for all this. But so are you, little girl. It's a two-way street. You and your mama are going to go see Jean at her office—" I turned to my wife. "When?" I asked.

"Tomorrow afternoon. Fourish," she said.

"Did you hear that?" I asked her. She nodded. I turned to Jewel. "Did you hear?" I demanded. Jewel nodded.

"Now, Mr. and Mrs. Shaunsee, I'm sorry you got caught up in all this. I'm sorry your boy did, too. I think it's time we all got home to our own beds and got some sleep."

The Shaunsees stood up, Mr. Shaunsee grabbing his son by the arm. Clifford gave Marlene a long last look good-bye and they headed out the door.

"Leonard, you need me to drive you back to Norman?" I asked.

"No, sir," he said. "I don't have any classes until late to-morrow. I'll get a ride back in the morning." I figured however he'd gotten involved in this was between him and his mother now.

I leaned down and kissed Marlene on the top of her head. She reached out for my hand and squeezed. Then I went over and kissed my sister on the head. She patted my hand, and I thought, my work here is done.

I went upstairs and got Johnny Mac and me and my family headed home.

I was late getting to the office the next morning, needless to say. I called in on my cell phone as I pulled out of the driveway and Gladys told me what was going on.

"Emmett's over with Dr. Jim getting the autopsy report on that girl from that church place. Dalton's out on a fender bender. Jasmine called in, said she'd come in if you need her."

"Call her back, tell her to get some rest. She was up late last night."

"Weren't we all?" Gladys said. I'd seen her and her husband and two of her boys in the crowd of volunteers the night before.

"I appreciate y'all coming out last night," I said.

Gladys made a humphing sound. "Just glad everything turned out all right. Hope that girl got the lickin' she deserved."

I wasn't about to debate child-rearing methods with my clerk; instead, I just said, "I'm on my way. See you in about twenty."

When I got there, Emmett was in my office, sitting in one of my two official visitor's chairs, his feet on my desk, perusing the autopsy report.

"Whatja got?" I asked.

"She was suffocated, Dr. Jim says."

"Suffocated? So all them wounds on the body were from the birds, huh?"

"Looks that way," Emmett said. He flipped a page. "Eighteen-year-old, healthy white female, no distinguishing marks—none, that is, except what the vultures put there."

"Could it have been an accident?" I asked.

"Like that sex thing you read about—where people hang

themselves or put plastic bags over their heads to get a better climax?"

I shuddered. "Don't seem like fun to me, but then I guess I'm just an old fuddy-duddy."

"Well, you are that, my man. But I gotta agree with you. Give me your basic old missionary position any old day."

"You think that's what this was?"

Emmett shrugged. "Well, she was naked. Coulda been. But then, where's the boy?"

"Exactly," I said. "You'd think he'd come in, all broke up, tell us what happened."

"Yeah, but maybe with his daddy on death row and all, he doesn't think he'd get a fair shake if it was some kind of kinky sex. You know, what with his daddy being a rapist and all."

I cringed at the thought of what Trent might or might not think about all that. But seeing as I was the man who put his daddy away, I might also be the last man on earth the boy would come to if he was in trouble.

"What did Dr. Jim say?" I asked.

"About what?"

"About the kinky sex thing."

"I don't know. I didn't ask him. Just now thought about it, tell you the truth."

I picked up the phone and dialed Dr. Jim's office number. He picked up on the second ring.

"What?"

"Hey, Doc, it's Milt."

"I got you the goddamn autopsy report. I'm busy. Leave me alone."

"Now, wait. Just a quick question. You think the girl suffocating could be, what do they call it, autoerotic asphyxiation?"

"Auto-what?"

"You know, people having sex, strangle or hang each other to get a better climax."

"That's sick, Milt," Dr. Jim said.

"I'm just asking—"

"Well, how would I know? Girl's got fiber and stuff under her fingernails, maybe some skin, I'm still checking. Seems if she wanted somebody to do this to her, she wouldn't a struggled, would she?"

"Well, if she realized it was getting too serious—"

"Whatever. Take your filthy mind elsewhere, Sheriff. I'm busy." And he hung up on me.

"She did have sex right before she died," Emmett said, studying the autopsy report.

"You know, it just doesn't make sense. They're leaving this religious retreat, right? They don't get as far as the fence and they're doing kinky sex?"

"Well, they were there for several days. Maybe the boy was kinda heated up."

"I don't know. I just don't like it."

"So what do you think happened?" Emmett asked.

I shrugged. "Damned if I know. All I *do* know is, we gotta find the boy before we find out anything else."

7

That afternoon I did something I thought I'd never do—I called my ex-wife. Now LaDonna and I didn't get along at the best of times, but she'd been real put off when Jean and I had gone and had Johnny Mac, proving once and for all it wasn't me shooting blanks that had kept us from having kids all those years we were married. LaDonna had always claimed to want a baby, but she'd never followed through, going to a fertility clinic or anything like that. She just up and said it was all my fault, and left it at that. But now I needed some information and she was the only one I knew who could give it to me.

She picked up on the third ring, sounding breathless. "LaDonna?" I asked.

"Yes?" she said, obviously not recognizing my voice, or pretending not to. For all the years, LaDonna reacted to most things like she had when I first met her—when she was a sophomore in high school.

"It's Milt," I said.

I'll give her credit—she didn't say "Milt who?"

"Why, my goodness, Milt. How are you? How's Joan?"

"Jean," I corrected. "And we're both fine. So's our little boy," I said, not being able to resist.

"Why are you calling?" she asked.

"Well, LaDonna, I got a case I think maybe you can help me with."

"Me? My goodness, Milt, I don't see how I can help you with anything *criminal*."

"Is it Bert or Barry owns the land out by the river?"

"Well, Bert owned about eight hundred acres, but he gave a hundred to each child. I think Barry's is on the south side of the river," she said. "But what does my brother or my nephew have to do with anything *criminal*?"

I figured ol' Bert must have had some problems with the IRS—the only reason I could see for that SOB to be giving anything away. Being a good cop, I answered her question with another question. "What do you know about this religious retreat Barry's got himself mixed up with?" I asked.

"The words you use, Milt. I swear! 'Mixed up.' Why, Barry found Jesus, I'm happy to say, and I don't really care how he did it. And that Brother Grigsby's the nicest man in the world. Bert wasn't exactly happy about Barry signing over the land to the church, but I felt it was a fine Christian gesture."

Not exactly happy, I thought. I almost giggled out loud at the thought of how "not exactly happy" my ex-brother-in-law was.

"You know how long ago this was?" I asked.

"That Barry gave the land to the church? Hm," she said, obviously thinking. "Well, he told us about it Christmas before last, but they'd been building on the land long before that. So, I'm not sure exactly when he signed the land over. What difference does it make, anyway? And why are you asking questions about Barry and the church? It's just like you to see foul play out of simple Christian charity!"

"There's been a murder up there," I said.

There was a long silence on the other end of the phone. Finally, in a small voice, she asked, "Is Barry okay?"

"Yeah, Barry's fine. It was a young woman—"

"Not Barry's little Ruth, was it?" she asked, breathless.

"No, hon—No, LaDonna, it wasn't Ruth," I said, embarrassed by my lapse into old familiarity. "It was a girl from Tejas County, come to spend some time at the retreat."

"Well, what happened?" she asked, her voice perking up when she realized it wasn't anything to do with her family.

"I'm still invest—"

"Still investigating," she interrupted. "I've heard that one about a million times."

"Well, it's true," I said defensively, what Jean would call "falling back into old patterns of behavior." "Look," I said, thinking it was about time I got off this particular phone call, "I thank you for your help, LaDonna. I gotta go."

"Well, next time you need to pick my brain, Mr. Sheriff, you just be sure to call," she said and hung up. Do I need to mention that it was said with a lot of sarcasm?

That evening after we'd eaten and gotten Johnny Mac off to bed, I asked Jean, "So did my sister and niece show up today?"

"Um-hum," she said, leafing through a medical journal that had come in the mail that day.

"So how'd it go?" I asked.

She laid the journal in her lap and looked at me over the top of her reading glasses. "You know I can't answer that," she said.

"Well, I mean, did they get along okay? Everything go smooth?"

She just looked at me and I felt a little like LaDonna must have felt earlier. Except not nearly so bitchy.

"Okay, okay," I said, going back to my copy of the *Longbranch Gazette*. "Forget I asked."

"Asked what?" she said, going back to her journal.

Sometimes it's no fun being kept out of the loop.

By the time I got to the office the next morning, there were three messages from Laura Johnson—excuse me, Laura Marshall. I'd almost been able to wipe that problem from my mind with all my family troubles, but somehow, like that ol' bad penny, Laura just kept popping up.

I took the three message slips back to my office and stared at them awhile. Finally, I picked up the phone and dialed.

"Hey, Miz Marshall," I said when she answered.

"I didn't hear from you yesterday at all!" she screeched. "Have you found my boy? What's going on? Milt, how can you treat me like this!"

"Whoa, now," I said. "Laura, just hold on. I'm not treating you any way. There's been nothing new to report on the investigation. When there is, you and Mr. Marshall will be the first people I call. As of right now, we're still checking leads."

"What leads?" she demanded.

Well, she had me there. I didn't have any; I just liked the way it sounded. "Nothing I can get into right now. But as soon as I find out anything, I'll call you—"

"No! You call me this afternoon! You let me know twice a day what's going on! That's the least you owe me!"

Well, that threw me. "Owe you? Ma'am, I don't owe you jackshit! If I recall, it's the other way around."

"That's why you're doing this, isn't it? You still hate *me* for what someone else did! I told you then and I'll tell you now. I was protecting my children. Which is exactly what I'm doing now! And you owe me, Milt Kovak, because for the first time in your sorry life, I made you feel alive!" And then she hung up.

I put the phone back in the cradle and leaned back in my chair. I wanted to throw things, yell at the top of my lungs, but that just isn't my style. Besides, I'd have three deputies and a clerk in my office so fast it would make my head swim. And my head was swimming enough as it was. Thank you very much.

I owed her. That's what she'd said. I owed her. For what? Making my gut hurt every time I thought of her? Coloring memories so black I'd need a flashlight to see them? For making me feel alive, she'd said. Well, that was a little bit true. I'd felt alive all right when I was with her. More alive than I'd ever felt before. And dead when it was over. I owed her that, too.

She seemed bound and determined to make this personal, the one thing I'd been trying to avoid since that first phone call. Personal was one thing I didn't want to get with Laura Johnson. I remembered all too well what personal had done to me the last time. Not to mention, I reminded myself sharply, the little fact of Jean and Johnny Mac.

The phone rang. After the second ring, I sighed real big and picked it up. "Kovak," I said.

"Sheriff, I got Mr. Marshall on the line for you," Gladys said.

"Put him through," I said, regretting the words even as they came out of my mouth.

"Kovak," I said again.

"Sheriff, this is Dixon Marshall."

"Yes, sir," I said. "I just spoke to your wife—"

"That's why I'm calling, Sheriff. I want to apologize for Laura's outburst."

How much of it did he hear? I wondered. How much did

he know? "No reason to apologize, Mr. Marshall," I said.

"I hope you understand how upset she is," he said. "To have no word of Trent for over a week has really gotten to her."

"I do understand that, Mr. Marshall. I have a son of my own. I can only imagine how hard this must be on y'all."

"The two younger kids are scared shitless, Sheriff, I can tell you that. And having their mother so upset is really getting to them. I know you're doing the best you can. All I ask is that you keep us posted."

"Yes, sir, I'll do that. And if y'all hear anything from Trent, no matter what, I want to be notified."

"Of course, Sheriff. And thanks for being so understanding. Bye," he said and hung up.

I said "bye" to an empty line. Oh, yeah, I was understanding, all right. I understood that Laura was in a jam again and it was me she expected to get her out of it. No matter what it did to me.

I took Emmett off what he was doing and had him join me once again for a go at the retreat. Emmett had the kind of mind I needed backing me up. Most police work isn't shoot-outs with bad guys—it's listening, finding the truth in the lies, and taking good notes, both on paper and in your head. Emmett was real good with recall. And the man took a mean note.

We headed toward the retreat, calling ahead so they'd let us in. It wasn't Barry this time manning the gate and the barbs, but a pregnant young woman who clasped her hands together in front of her forehead and bowed at her waist as we drove through. I had an inclination to bow back but managed to stifle it.

Nothing much had changed at the compound. Few more people bustling about, mostly women, a lot of 'em pregnant, carrying laundry baskets full of this and that. A man was hammering on something near the sanctuary, another on the roof, laying tar paper. Everyone we saw was dressed as Barry had been, in those Gandhi-type pajamas, although the crosses around the necks of the people we saw were smaller and made of wood instead of the silver of Barry's and the gold of Brother Grigsby's.

We pulled up in front of the pavilion as Barry came out of the sanctuary building. We got out of the car and met him at one of the tables, already laden with glasses of lemonade.

He bowed, then said, "Please, sit, gentlemen. Have some refreshment. How can I be of service today?"

"We were hoping to talk to Brother Grigsby," I said.

"I'm so sorry, Sheriff, but our Light is at prayer right now."

"And when will he be finished?" I asked.

"In his own time," Barry said and smiled.

I had an overwhelming need to wipe the smile off his face but managed to restrain myself. "That's all well and good, Barry," I said, smiling back, "but we need to speak to him now."

"Is there anything I can help you with?" Barry asked, leaning forward and looking very sincere. Having known the kid since he was a pup, I knew just how sincere he was. That is, not much.

"I appreciate your offer, Barry," I said, matching insincere sincerity breath for breath, "but we really need to talk to the man in charge."

"I *am* in charge when our Light is absent," Barry said, smiling.

"Fine," I said. "I wanna see this place. Every bit of it." I pointed toward the tents. "That where Trent and the girl stayed?" I asked.

"The one on the right is the men's dormitory and the one on the left is the women's. But I can't let you go there, Sheriff,"

91

he said, shaking his head and smiling. "It would be an invasion of our flock's privacy."

"Don't look to me like they have much privacy," Emmett remarked.

"Then it would be a shame to invade what little they have," Barry shot back.

"Yeah, it's a shame," I agreed, standing up, "but it's gotta be done."

Barry stood, too. "Nothing of Amanda's is there, Sheriff. She and Trent packed their things when they left."

"Well, you never know," I said. "I might find something useful under her bed or in the trash can or something."

"The dorms are thoroughly cleaned on a daily basis," Barry said, again the smile in place.

"And the trash?"

"We burn it daily."

"Really covering your tracks, huh?" Emmett said.

"Pardon?" Barry asked, the smile gone, replaced by a quizzical frown.

"I think I'd like to take a look anyhow," I said.

Barry smiled again. "I'm afraid I can't allow that, Sheriff. You will need the express permission of Brother Grigsby, and as I said, he's at prayer right now."

"So you aren't that much in charge?" I asked.

He smiled. "Our Light, Brother Grigsby, is the only true leader, of this retreat and our spiritual beings, Sheriff. It is for him to decide if nonbelievers are allowed to befoul our sacred space."

I laughed. "That's good, Barry. You learn that talk at Vacation Bible School?"

The smile vanished. "Milt, I'm trying to be nice here. You're not helping. Y'all are gonna have to leave, right now. Unless you have a warrant?"

I didn't have one and doubted I could get one. "When do you expect Brother Grigsby to be through praying?" I asked.

"As I said before, Sheriff, our Light keeps his own time with our Lord and Saviour."

"Yeah, whatever," I said, and headed for the Jeep. I was getting real tired of the Light and all his little rays of sunshine.

When I got back to the sheriff's department there was a surprise waiting for me in my office.

"Hey, what're you doing here?" I asked, leaning down to kiss my niece on the forehead.

"Hi, Uncle Milt. I hope I'm not disturbing you?"

"Not at all, honey. But don't you have school?"

"Teacher day. We got out at noon. Some kind of conference."

"Well, I'm usually not one to look a gift horse in the mouth, but I still gotta ask. What brings you to see me?"

Marlene lowered her head, not meeting my eyes. "I wanted to apologize," she said.

"Honey, no need for that—"

She looked up. "Yes, there is. I was a real bitch to you, Uncle Milt. And you've never been anything but good to me. So I apologize."

"Aunt Jean making you do this?" I asked.

Marlene grinned. "Well, she did suggest I had some apologizing to do to a lot of people. I just decided to put you first on my list."

"What about your mama?"

Marlene rolled her eyes. "All right, second on my list. I already apologized to her. No, third. I apologized to Aunt Jean, too. Oh, and Harmon. I guess that puts you—"

I laughed. "It's okay, honey, it's okay. Long as I'm in the top hundred."

She laughed along with me, then sobered. "I'm serious, Uncle Milt. I know I've been behaving like a baby, and hurting a lot of people, and I apologize. I think it had a lot to do with Leonard going off to college. It was almost like losing Daddy all over again, I guess."

I could see my wife's fine hand in this thinking, and was glad the girl was realizing she had some problems to solve. "Well, I accept your apology, Marlene," I said formally.

She grinned. "Thanks, Uncle Milt." She sat still for a moment, then looked at me. "That girl you were talking about? The one who got killed? What happened?"

"Honey, we don't need to get into—"

"I really need to know, Uncle Milt."

"You know about cults and the like?" I asked.

She rolled her eyes. Marlene was real good about letting you know when you asked a stupid question. "Yes! Was she involved with something like that? Here?" she asked, incredulous to think that something as far out as a cult could be anywhere near Prophesy County—sort of the way I thought a little over a week ago.

"Yeah, seems we got one. Far as I can tell, they seem to be mixing up Christianity with a little Hindu, and maybe a little bit of *Star Trek*."

"Jeez! Out here? You wouldn't think something like that would want to be way out here in the boonies."

"Land's cheap," I suggested. Real cheap in this case, I thought.

She shrugged. "Yeah. I suppose. But what has that got to do with the girl who got murdered?"

"She and her boyfriend went to this retreat, first for the weekend, then to stay awhile. The people at the retreat say the two decided to leave after less than a week—the boy's idea more than the girl's. The next day her body was found

94

in a pasture, naked and dead. The boy hasn't been seen since."

"You think he did it?" she asked. "The boyfriend?"

I shrugged. "I don't know. I can tell you this, though. Something ain't kosher at that retreat, I can guaran-damn-tee you that."

"What makes you say that?"

"They're secretive. Which makes sense with any cult. They gotta have their secrets. But there's just something not right there. Can't put my finger on it."

"How did these kids get involved in the first place?" she asked.

"Hanging out with the wrong crowd. Houseful of wanna-be cult groupies and computer freaks in Taylor." I laughed. "The one I talked to was named Naomi Woman, if you can believe it."

"Naomi Woman?" Marlene laughed back. "You think she made that up?"

We grinned at each other. It felt good talking to my niece like this. She was a good sounding board, helping me to piece together some of what I was thinking.

"One thing really bothers me about that place," I said. "More'n half the women I've seen there are pregnant. And way more'n half of the people at that retreat are women. More like three-quarters."

"And they're all pregnant?"

"Not all. But a bunch of them."

"Jeez, Uncle Milt. That's weird."

"That's what I'm telling you," I said. "Something's wrong at that place and I wish I could figure out what it is."

I was halfway home when I got a call from Gladys. "Milt, we got a report of a sexual assault in progress at the Baghdad Apartments. That's on your way home, idn't it?"

"Yeah," I said, sighing.

"Thing is, got a wreck on the highway, everybody's tied up. And this girl was some upset, Milt. I could hardly understand her."

"What's the address?" I asked. With a rape in progress, I needed to get the lead out.

The Baghdad Apartments were a group of fourplexes nestled around a defunct swimming pool with about two feet of water left in it and a lot of garbage floating about. They weren't the cheapest housing in the county, but pretty damn close to it.

I got to the apartment complex, gun drawn, found the right unit, and kicked the cheap apartment door open with the heel of my boot. Four young men were sitting around on sofas and chairs watching a ball game on ESPN, beers in hand.

"What the fuck?" one said, jumping up from a recliner.

"Where is she?" I demanded, pointing my gun at the young man.

"Who?" he asked.

"The girl that called in the rape report."

The standing young man sat back down. "Oh, for Christ's sake. Yvette?" he called over his shoulder. "Get your butt out here!"

A girl came out of the bedroom, followed by a young man tucking in his shirttail. The girl had a lot of curly black hair going down almost to her waist, and I could've bet you the hair weighed more than the rest of her body. That was one skinny young lady.

"Ma'am, are you okay?" I asked.

She spread her arms out dramatically, encompassing all the young men present. "They rape me!" she declared in a heavy accent.

"All of 'em?" I asked.

"All of dem! They rape me!"

I holstered my gun. Looking at the young man behind her, I said, "What's going on here?"

He shrugged. "I dunno," he said, looking at the floor.

"What's your name?" I asked the girl.

"Ees Yvette."

"Yvette what?" I asked.

"No what. Jeest Yvette."

"What's your last name?" I asked, enunciating each word clearly.

"No lass name. Ees Yvette."

I looked at the boy behind her. He sighed. "Maladondo," he said.

"Did these men have sexual intercourse with you against your wishes, Ms. Maladondo?"

"They rape me! All dem!"

"Like I'd touch *her*," the boy in the recliner said. "With a ten-foot pole and a three-foot Czech." The other three laughed and there was a lot of high-fiving going on.

I looked at the young man who had followed Yvette out of the bedroom. "What's your name?" I asked.

"Truman Conchfeld, sir," he said. "And that's my brother Sherman," he said, pointing to the boy in the recliner.

"And the others?"

"Mickey Donley, Big Bob Lloyd and Little Bob Michaels."

Mickey and the Big and Little Bobs waved their arms in greeting, kinda like a roll call.

"Did you guys rape this girl?" I asked the room in general.

A chorus of noes rang out. I looked at Truman Conchfeld.

"Yvette's my girlfriend, officer," he said. "She tends to get upset with me and exaggerates some."

"Tell him about the time she peed on the couch!" his brother Sherman called out.

"Or the time she tried to commit suicide by drinking Comet!" Big Bob added and they all laughed.

"See?" Yvette cried, clutching her hands together and wringing them for all they were worth. "You see how they treat me? Ees rape ees what eet ees! They rape my soul!"

I asked the young woman and her boyfriend to step outside with me.

"You're gonna have to get this door fixed, Truman," I said. "The county's not paying for that."

"Yes, sir, officer," he said, hanging his head.

"I'm the sheriff, son," I said.

Truman looked even more crestfallen, if that was possible.

"The door, eet ees broke when you rescue me, yes?" Yvette said, grabbing my arm and looking up into my eyes.

"Ma'am," I said, disengaging myself from her grip, "you called in a false police report. That's against the law—"

"Ees not false!" she cried, clutching her concave chest. "They treat me so bad! I feel like rape!"

"Ma'am, rape is a criminal offense and it means something particular. It doesn't mean that somebody's hurt your feelings. Now I'm not gonna take you in this time, but young lady, I want you to listen, and listen good. No more false police reports, you understand?"

I looked at the boyfriend. "Think you can keep her calm?" I asked.

He looked at me and a more pitiful look I've never seen on a man's face. "I doubt it," he said.

I patted his arm. "Just give it your best shot, son," I said, and headed for the Jeep and home.

And I would've made it, too, except I stopped at a Kwik Stop for a carton of milk. If it hadn't been for that, I would have been out of range and Gladys wouldn't have been able to reach me when the second call came in from the Baghdad Apartments.

"What is it this time, Gladys?" I asked.

"That same girl, Milt. The one with the accent? She's calling in a drug report. Says there's dope all over the apartment."

"Oh, for God's sake," I said.

"Well, Milt, dope's dope, right?"

"Right." I sighed. "I'm heading there now."

I turned my Jeep around and headed back to the Baghdad. Since it had only been half an hour since my last visit, the broken door was leaning against the jamb, leaving a man-sized space for entrance. I knocked on the jam and entered, not waiting for a response.

"Hey, Sheriff," Sherman called from the recliner. "What brings you back?"

"Drugs," I said.

All four boys looked up. "No drugs here," one of the Bobs said.

"Absolutely," Mickey agreed. He held up his Bud Lite. "Our drug of choice, Sheriff."

Truman came out of the bedroom, looking hangdogged. "Sheriff, can I help you?"

"Truman, we got another call from your girlfriend. She says there are drugs here."

The girl stuck her head out from the bedroom. "No, I say no such thing."

"Young lady, if you got me over here on another wild-goose chase, I'm putting your butt in the slam, and I'm not kidding around."

Yvette stepped out into the room, her hands behind her back. With a flourish, she brought both hands in front, showing off tiny marijuana plants, roots and all. "Eet's too, eet's too!" she said. "Dey got drugs! Big-time! See?"

I looked at Truman and the other four boys. "They're mine, Sheriff," Truman said. "I was growing them in my closet with a grow light. None of these guys even knew about it."

He held his arms up in front of him. "Take me away, sir," he said.

By the look on his face I decided arresting him was the biggest favor I could do him. So I cuffed him and read him his rights, took the plants from the girl's hands and led poor Truman out the door.

"Son," I said, once we were alone in the car, Truman sitting shotgun since I wasn't in a patrol car, "how did you hook up with that young lady?"

"Known her since high school," he said. He looked at me out of the corner of his eye. "Her mother's LouAnne Slawson, owns the Cut and Curl in Longbranch?"

I nodded. "I know LouAnne, I went to high school with her. She was a few years behind, but she certainly wasn't, you know, foreign," I said, for want of a better word.

Truman laughed ruefully. "Oh, the accent. Maladondo was her father's name, although I don't think Yvette ever actually met him. But she likes doing accents. This month she's doing Spanish. Six weeks ago it was English. I think her Spanish's better."

"Son," I said, shaking my head, "you could do better. Well, if not better, at least saner."

"Yes, sir," he said, "but I love her."

I nodded. There was no arguing with that.

I did the paperwork, booking poor Truman on misdemeanor drug charges. I planned on having a talk with the judge on the young man's behalf. No way should this kid do time for two runty little marijuana plants and an insane girlfriend.

It had started raining while I was booking poor Truman and by the time I left, it was a steady downpour. Once again I got back in the Jeep and headed for my mountain. And once again I didn't get any farther than the Baghdad Apartments.

As I passed I saw a great conflagration. One that definitely shouldn't be there. I drove up and parked the Jeep, got out in the rain and headed for the swimming pool. Sherman Conchfeld was standing in the pouring rain next to the swimming pool, staring at the fire, a can of gasoline by his side. It appeared to be a pair of boots ablaze, women's boots if I could be so bold as to guess, and the toes were beginning to curl up like the feet of the Wicked Witch of the East.

"Sherman," I said, staring at the fire.

"Sir," he said, not taking his eyes off it.

"What you burning?" I asked conversationally.

"Her boots," Sherman said.

"Yvette's?" I asked.

Sherman looked up and grinned. "Yeah, she just bought 'em yesterday. Paid two hundred dollars. She's up in the apartment right now, looking all over the place for 'em."

"Well, make sure you put the fire out when they're done," I said.

"Yes, sir," Sherman said, and I left him to it.

With all the excitement at the Baghdad, I'd forgotten to call home, tell Jean I was gonna be late. With LaDonna, this would have led to hysterics; with my old girlfriend Glenda Sue, I would have gotten a raised eyebrow and a guilt trip. With Jean, I got a lecture.

"If we respect one another, Milt," she said, slamming my cold plate of dinner down on the table, "we notify each other if we're not going to be where we say we're going to be when we say we're going to be there. Not doing so shows a lack of respect, not only to me as your wife, worried about you and your line of work, but it shows a lack of respect to me as a human being, your equal and your partner."

"I'm sorry," I said.

"Not to mention your son," she said, pouring iced tea into a glass and slamming it down in front of me—I could've got my own food, I usually do, but I think all the slamming made her feel better. "Don't you think he worries? Of course he's only two," she said, as if in answer to something I'd said, "but you have no idea how early children grasp these things. I'm tense, Milton. Having your mother tense makes a child tense. Do you understand anything I'm saying to you?"

"Yes, I do. You're right. I'm sorry."

She sighed. "You're not listening to a word I'm saying, are you?"

I thought it was a rhetorical question, so I took a bite of food instead of answering.

"I knew you weren't listening!" she said, and slammed into the bedroom.

I just kept on eating, knowing I was going to need all the strength I had to get through the evening to come. Marriage is scary business.

Truman Conchfeld was sleeping soundly when I peeked in on him the next morning. It wasn't exactly a smile on his face, but it was definitely a look of contentment. I wondered if maybe this was the first full night's sleep the boy'd had since hooking up with little Miz Yvette. No accounting for love, I thought, shaking my head and thinking about my own long night the night before. Jean's not an easy woman to get around, but there is this spot, on her neck, a little south of her left ear . . .

I found Emmett in his office and plopped down in his visitor's chair. (I have two, he only has one. Not that I'm counting, or anything.)

"What's up?" he asked.

"You meet our guest?" I said, pointing toward the cells.

"Saw him, but he's been asleep."

Briefly I told him of the events of the previous evening. Emmett grinned. "Poor guy," he said.

I told him about Sherman and the boots and he laughed out loud. "Unfortunately, his brother probably paid for 'em," Emmett surmised.

"I hadn't thought of that," I said, shaking my head. "You're probably right."

"So anything new on the Amanda Nederwald thing?" he asked me.

I shook my head. "We gotta find the boy," I said. "He's the key to the whole thing. Either he killed her or he knows who did."

"You think he's hiding out?"

"If he did it, yeah. But if he didn't . . ."

"You think he's dead, too?" Emmett asked.

I shrugged. "I think that possibility is very real," I said.

"And if both the kids are dead, you're thinking something definitely happened at that retreat?"

"It's crossed my mind," I admitted. "Something ain't kosher up there," I said, repeating the thought I'd shared with Marlene.

"I'll agree with that, but I'm not so sure they'd go so far as to kill two kids. I mean, Milt, why?"

"Well, that's the sixty-four-thousand-dollar question, don't you think? Why would anybody do it? Unless we're talking drive-by serial killer or something, and if we are we'll never know."

"And in the meantime?" Emmett asked.

"In the meantime," I said, getting up and stretching, "I gotta go talk to Judge Mason about poor Truman. And while I've got his interest, I just might see what we can do about finding out a little more about the old Seven Trumpets."

Judge Jeffrey Mason was a relatively young guy, which basically means he was younger than me. Somewhere in his mid-forties, maybe. You know, young. Truman Conchfeld sat on a bench in the judge's courtroom while I stood by the judge's bench, telling him the woeful story of poor Truman and his crazy girlfriend.

Jeff just shook his head. "Think of any charges for this girl?"

"Well, no, sir," I said. "I let her have that first false police report, and I hate going back on my word."

He looked out at the young man sitting with his head bent, staring at his shoes. "Mr. Conchfeld," the judge called out.

Truman shot to his feet, a look of fright on his face. "Yes, sir?" he asked.

"Approach the bench." To me, he said, "Stay here, Sheriff."

"Yes, sir," I said.

Truman got up to the bench, hands straight to his sides, his eyes big.

"Sheriff Kovak here ran you, young man, and you appear to have a clean record."

"Oh, yes, sir, I do, sir. Your Honor, sir."

"Son, you ever think about finding you a new lady friend?" the judge asked.

Truman lowered his head. "I love her, sir."

"You know I can't recommend what somebody do with their love life, Mr. Conchfeld, but it seems to me that if I were in your shoes, I'd figure out some way to get as far from this young lady as possible. You understand the position she's put

104

you in, Mr. Conchfeld? And not only you, son, but the sheriff here and me."

Truman nodded. "Yes, sir," he said, dejected.

The judge looked up and spied a defense attorney heading out the door of the courtroom. "Roy!" he called. "Come here a minute."

The attorney stopped and turned, his shoulders sagging because he hadn't actually made the door, and came down the aisle. "Your Honor?" he asked.

"This young man needs an attorney," the judge said. "Yolanda," he said, addressing the clerk, "put Roy Higgins here down as Mr. Conchfeld's attorney of record. That okay with you, Roy?"

"Certainly, Your Honor."

"Mr. Conchfeld," the judge said, "go have a seat while I talk with your attorney."

"Yes, sir, Your Honor, sir," Truman said, making a beeline for the courtroom benches.

"Roy, you don't need to know the details, suffice it to say me and the sheriff here think this boy's got a rotten deal. I want you to plead him time served and we'll dicker on probation, okay?"

"Yes, Your Honor," Roy said, shooting me a look.

I mouthed, "Tell you later," while the judge called Truman back to the stand.

"Your Honor," Roy said, "my client pleads guilty and we ask that you sentence him to time served, no probation."

"I'll go with time served," the judge said, "five years probation."

"One year, please, Your Honor."

"Two," the judge said and banged his gavel.

Without a word to his client, Roy Higgins walked out of the courtroom. Truman stood there looking dumb and I pulled him by the arm, leading him out of the courtroom.

"What happened?" he asked once we were in the hall.

"You need to go see the county clerk, sign up for probation. You'll be on probation for two years, which means you better not be growing any more marijuana plants in your closet."

"Yes, sir! I mean, no sir!"

"Whatever. Time served means that last night's all the jail time you're gonna do. Now, have you been thinking about this relationship you got with Yvette?"

Truman sighed. "Yes, sir, I'm thinking maybe it's time I went to stay with my cousin in Tulsa. If I can leave town."

"Leaving town's fine, son, but stay in the state, just to keep all our *i*'s dotted and our *t*'s crossed. You understand?"

"Yes, sir," he said. He held out his hand and I took it and he shook it like a pump handle. "Sheriff, I know you're the one who talked to the judge on my behalf, and sir, well . . ."

There were tears in his eyes. This I could not handle. "Get you a new girlfriend, son," I said, patted him on the back and left him standing in the hall of the courthouse.

"Something's not kosher out at that place," Marlene said.

"What's 'kosher'?" Clifford asked.

"You know, not right. Something's not right out there."

"Like what?" he asked, his hand caressing her knee.

It was a pretty day, spring all around. They sat on a blanket under the Derry Creek Bridge, katydids making music around them, birds singing in the trees.

Marlene pushed his hand off her knee. "Don't," she said absently. "It's just—I don't know, Clifford. Uncle Milt thinks something's wrong at that place. He thinks those people may have had more to do with this girl's murder than the guy did. You know, her boyfriend."

Clifford sighed. "So what does this have to do with us?" he asked, his hand reaching for her shoulder.

Marlene let him pull her toward him and returned his kiss, retreating as his tongue headed her way. "Don't, Clifford. I'm serious here!"

"About what?" Clifford said, exasperated.

"I think we should help Uncle Milt," Marlene said, her eyes bright.

"Help him how?" Clifford asked, his mind retreating from the idea as his body retreated from hers.

"I know who to contact to get into that place—"

"Into it? Why in the world would we do that? Marlene! Get serious!"

"I am serious," she said. "Uncle Milt needs someone on the inside. Who could be better for the job than us?"

Clifford scrambled to his feet. "Whoa, now, Marlene, hold on! I'm not going to risk my neck—"

"Clifford," Marlene asked, her voice small and sounding wounded, "don't you love me?"

8

I met Roy Higgins for lunch at the Longbranch Inn. Over chicken-fried steak, skin-on mashed potatoes, green beans with bacon and a side of fried okra, cornbread, and a mason jar of iced tea, I told him the sad story of Truman Conchfeld.

Roy laughed and shook his head. "Well, glad I could be of service," he said. Roy was my age and twice my girth. His chins shook when he laughed and his eyes were getting lost behind the fat of his cheeks. His blond hair was thinning on top even quicker than mine, and the brown suit he wore was a little too short in the arms and legs. By all accounts he was a good lawyer who had moved to Longbranch twenty years ago from Oklahoma City for the quiet country life.

Changing the subject, he asked, "What's up with this dead girl out at the Seven Trumpets?"

"You know the place?" I asked, he being the first person outside of the place or its groupies I'd heard use the rightful name.

"Yeah, I handled the paperwork on the transfer of owner-ship a while back," he said. "I'd been doing work now and again for Bert Leventhwart, so when his kid asked me to handle the paperwork, I thought no sweat. Two days later your ex-brother-in-law calls me up cussing and screaming and said he wouldn't do business with me again if I was the last lawyer alive in Oklahoma."

"Good ol' Bert," I said.

Roy grinned. "A prince among men."

"So when was this?" I asked. "That you did the deed transfer?"

Roy thought for a moment. "About a year ago, I guess. Maybe nine months. Why?"

I shrugged. "No reason, really. Just found myself interested in the place, is all."

" 'Cause of the girl dying up there. Those freakoids responsible, you think?" he asked.

"Why do you call them freakoids?"

"I take it you *have* met the good Brother Grigsby?" Roy asked.

"Oh, yeah, I met him."

"Then why else do you think I call them freakoids? A whole bunch of people hanging on the very word of that jerk-off? What a crock! That guy's as slimy as a squashed slug!"

"You'll get no argument from me," I said. "But I wouldn't mind a whole lot if you decided to get real specific with regard to Brother Grigsby."

Roy grinned. "Oh, goody," he said. "He's a suspect."

I gave him my best "I'm the sheriff, don't mess with me" look, and said, "Everybody's a suspect right now, Roy."

Somehow that didn't wipe the grin off Roy's face. "Well, I'll tell you. I was suspicious of the fella from the get-go. He comes waltzing into my office with Barry, both of 'em wearing those silly white PJ things, and he just smarms up the place, right off the bat. Glad-handing me, coming on like gangbusters to poor ol' Bobbie at my front desk. I thought maybe he had a convert right there, but she managed to get over it.

"Anyway, he's going on and on about the generous offer that 'Brother' Barry's making to the church and all, but funny thing, the deed doesn't go into the name of the church, it goes to the name of Theodore Davis Grigsby. Right there in my office he hands Barry a dollar bill for payment on this land and they both laugh like it's the funniest thing ever. I gotta admit I never much liked Bert, but I had to agree with him on his boy giving that land away. That land is worth close to a million being right there on the river. You know how waterfront real estate is moving these days."

"The land's in Grigsby's name, not the church?"

"That's right," Roy said. "Tell me that's not suspicious."

"Did you ever go out there?" I asked.

"Naw, I stayed as far away from the place as I could. But I'll tell you this. I guess I'm just not a trusting soul, so I had Bobbie do a little investigative work on the Internet, and guess what?"

"What?" I asked.

"Theodore Davis Grigsby never existed before 1985. The social security number was issued in 1985."

"In Colorado?" I asked, remembering what little Grigsby had told me of his past.

Roy frowned. "No, it wasn't Colorado," he said. "Somewhere in the South, I think. I can't remember but I can sure have Bobbie look it up again."

We finished our lunches, topped them off with a piece of pecan pie for me and a slab of strawberry shortcake for Roy, both of us promising not to tell our wives what we had for lunch, then headed for his office, which was walking distance from the Longbranch Inn.

The Law Offices of Roy Higgins, as the sign on the marquee declared them, were on the second floor of the Longbranch National Bank building. I hadn't been in that building for a while since my ex-wife had married Dwayne Dickey, the bank's president, who's just about the biggest asshole the world has ever produced. The entrance to the upstairs offices was from a side door next to the bank's big double doors, so we didn't have to go into the bank itself to gain access. We took the stairs up, with me following Roy, and a little worried about the heart attack he was bound to have one of these days, especially climbing those steep stairs. I was just praying he didn't have it right then and fall backward on me.

His office was the second one from the landing and had the name THE LAW OFFICES OF ROY HIGGINS stenciled on the frosted glass panel set into the heavy oak door. The Long-branch National Bank building was an old one, with twelve-foot ceilings, transoms over the doors, and moldings that would put an antique dealer into cardiac arrest. The front room was large, with big, comfortable-looking armchairs for clients and an old teacher's desk by the back wall, where the infamous Bobbie and her computer sat.

The lady in question could have been anywhere from twelve to twenty-five. The low estimate came from the two braids hanging down either side of her head and the bangs cut straight across her forehead; the high estimate from the almost invisible crow's feet around her eyes. She was dressed in jeans and a blue T-shirt with an American flag on the front, showing off perky breasts and when she stood up, a nice round little butt. Her face was freckled and appeared makeup-free, and her smile was as straight and white as a toothpaste model's. Her voice, when she spoke, was high and lilting, and I couldn't help hoping her age was lower than twenty-five so I could introduce her to my nephew Leonard.

"Hey, Mr. Higgins," she said, bouncing up. "You've got lots of messages!"

"Anything important?" Roy asked.

"Well, your wife," she said and giggled.

"I said 'anything important,'" Roy said, grinning back. Then, to me, he said, "She's mean as a snake, my wife, but she's all mine. Excuse me while I call her back and get my butt-chewing of the day."

He left me alone in the outer office with Bobbie.

"You're the sheriff, aren't you?" she said, breathless.

"Yes, ma'am, I am," I said, grinning at her. You couldn't help grinning at her.

She held out her hand and I shook it. "I'm Bobbie Turnball, Mr. Higgins's executive assistant," she said.

"Does that pay more than secretary?" I asked.

She grinned. "Ten more cents an hour," she said. "And I got cards!"

Roy came out of his office. "I forgot to feed the dog this morning. According to my wife, he almost died. Also, I left a window open and the alarm off, which means, of course, that I'm planning on having her killed." He grinned. "She's a pip, my wife."

Jean and I had met Liz Higgins several times at different functions. She was as petite as her husband was large and the sweetest lady you'd ever want to meet. Jean couldn't stand her.

Roy turned to Bobbie. "Remember a while back when I had you look up that stuff on that Brother Grigsby character?" he asked her.

She nodded and shuddered. "What a scary guy," she said.

"Can you find that stuff on the Internet again?" he asked.

"Well, sure, Mr. Higgins, but I printed it out if you'd rather just see the file."

She deftly turned to a filing cabinet, opened it, put her finger immediately on the right file, and pulled it out, handing it to Roy.

113

"See why I keep her around?" he asked me.

Roy took the file back to his office and I followed him. He sat down on a sofa, leaving room for me, and spread the file out on the coffee table. We both took out reading glasses.

Not only were the hard copies of the Internet sheets in the file, but Bobbie had typed up a report that put everything in perspective. According to the report, the name "Theodore Davis Grigsby" appeared on no DMV listings or social security listings until 1985, when a card was issued in that name out of the Social Security office in Baton Rouge, Louisiana. The name "Alma Grigsby," Brother Grigsby's wife, first appeared on a Social Security listing in 1990, out of an office in Denver, Colorado, and, by cross-referencing, Bobbie had discovered that Theodore Davis Grigsby and Alma Smith had married in Denver in early 1990. According to Bobbie's report, she could find no social security or DMV listing for an Alma Smith in that area.

Reading my mind, Roy called Bobbie into his office.

"Any way we can trace Alma? Thinking, of course, of Smith as an alias?"

Bobbie stood there a moment, frowning, the crow's feet around her eyes deepening and ruining my chance of introducing her to my nephew. "Well," she finally said, "this is a cult, right? So, it stands to reason—" She snapped her fingers and ran back to her area. Roy and I followed her while she moved her computer screen to an Internet connection.

She got on what she called a search engine and started looking for "clubs." "There are all sorts of clubs on the Internet," she said. "I found out this trick a while back when I was trying to figure out if this guy I was seeing had a record— Anyway, that's neither here nor there. See what we do—Ah." She pulled up a group named "Cult Survivors." "Let's see if they have a chat room. That would be the quickest way. Otherwise, we'll have to wait for e-mails, and you know, that could take, like, hours."

I tried not to think about things like, you know, mail, and how long that used to take. I know, I'm an old fogy.

"Ooo, they have one. Let's see if anyone's talking." She got a screen up that had words scrolling across. "Couple of people here. Let's just lurk for a while, see what's going on."

After a few minutes of reading what appeared to be just friendly banter, Bobbie said, "I think I need to interrupt this chatter. They're going nowhere." She typed in, "Hey, guys, need some help." Pushed a key and it came up on the screen, with Bobbie's name listed as "Lawsweetie." In seconds there was a response from "Newbetter." "Hey, Lawsweetie, welcome. What's your question?"

"Need some 411 on a guy named Theodore Davis Grigsby, calls himself Brother Grigsby, married to a woman used to be called Alma Smith."

A response came from someone called "473cultless." "Used to be Alma Taggert in Denver area. Heard she hooked up w/ some x-con—could be Grigsby—don't remember name. Taggert was real ballbuster, I hear."

"Ask him what Taggert looked like," I told Bobbie. She typed in the question.

"Wimpy little thing—dishwater-blond, skinny. Mean mouth."

"Sounds like our Sister Alma," I told Bobbie and Roy. "Ask what she was doing as Taggert."

Bobbie typed in the question and Newbetter answered. "She the one had that motor home to Jesus?"

"That's the one," 473cultless answered. "Used to take in underage kids and the parents had to pay to get them back. Think that was in NV. She got out of there by the skin on her nonexistent ass. Last I heard she was in CO."

"Ask them to check with anybody else in the club, see what they can find. Have 'em e-mail you," I suggested.

Bobbie typed in, "Please, please, please, need all the 411 I can get on Taggert, Smith, or Grigsby. Ask the group and e-mail me????"

Newbetter answered, "What's going on? Something we need to know?"

Bobbie typed in, "When I find out I'll let you know. Meanwhile????"

473cultless typed in, "We're having a meeting tomorrow night. Newbetter and I will quiz the group and one of us will get back to you."

Bobbie typed, "1000 thanks." She gave them her e-mail address and disconnected from the chat room.

"Well, well, well," Roy said. "Interesting."

I grinned at Bobbie. "How old are you?" I asked.

"I'll be twenty my next birthday," she said.

My grin got bigger. "I have this nephew . . ."

I spent the afternoon listening to Jasmine Bodine whine about the hookers.

"I can't figure out where they're taking their tricks, Milt," she said.

"You've been tailing 'em?"

"I try," she whined. "Twice I tried. But both times I lost 'em."

"Can you get close enough to hear a deal going down?"

"I think they figured me out, Milt. They never talk to a john when I'm around."

I thought for a minute. "What do you wear when you go to the bar, Jasmine?"

She gave me a look. "Not my uniform, if that's what you're thinking!"

I grinned. "I surely hope not. But what kind of clothes?"

She shrugged. "I dunno," she whined. "The usual. Jeans and a T-shirt."

"What does the T-shirt say?" I asked.

Her eyes got big, then narrowed. "Nothing," she said, her tone shifting from whiny to evasive.

I grinned at her again. "It's not your Academy T-shirt, is it?" I asked.

"No! It's the one that says, 'Next time you get mugged, call a hippie.'"

"Not a great idea, Jasmine."

She sighed. "I wasn't thinking."

"You got a wig?" I asked.

"No. Why would I?" she asked, fingering her hair as if I'd found it wanting.

"Get some petty cash from Gladys and go get you a wig and some slinky clothes and more makeup if you need it. Trash yourself up and go back. Maybe they won't recognize you."

"Trash myself up?" she asked.

I sighed. "Like a hooker, Jasmine. You know, protective coloration."

Jasmine's set her lips in a prim line. "I'm not sure about this, Milt."

"Jasmine, you're my only female deputy. And I just can't see Dalton looking good in drag."

Jasmine actually laughed at the thought. Then she sighed and stood up. "Okay. I'll try," she whined, and left my office.

Emmett replaced her in the doorway. "Got a visitor out at Gladys's desk," he said.

"Who's that?"

"Becca Tatum. The Nederwald girl's mother."

"Oh, Christ," I said, putting my face into my hands, elbows

117

resting on my desk. "Send her back," I said, taking a deep breath.

"She's not alone, Milt. Got a lawyer with her," Emmett said as he left.

And she did indeed have a lawyer with her. His name was Ashton Simon Blakeley, Ass to those who knew him best, and he was the former county, attorney for Prophesy County. He had been a pain in *my* ass the entire eight years he was head lawyer for the county, and when he left under a cloud of suspicion, which he felt was all my fault, he became worse. Luckily I had little to do with him nowadays, as he mostly did wills and divorces.

I stood up as they entered, extending my hand to Mrs. Tatum. "Ma'am, it's good to see you again. Wish it was under better circumstances. Please have a seat."

"Sheriff, this is my lawyer, Mr. Blakeley," Becca Tatum said, taking one of the visitor's chairs while Ass took the other.

"We know each other," I said, not extending my hand to Ass. I doubted that he'd shake it.

"Mrs. Tatum contacted me because she felt you weren't doing enough about the murder of her daughter, Sheriff. I'm with her today mainly on a fact-finding mission, to see what progress you've made and find out why you haven't kept her in the loop. I understand you have been keeping the parents of the boy who probably *did* this well informed."

"We have no idea who *did* this at the moment, Mr. Blakeley. And as for the parents of the boy who is missing, they've been calling me to see what's going on. Best of my knowledge, your client has not contacted this office. Until today, of course."

"That's neither here nor there, Sheriff. Please tell us what's going on with the investigation."

"All I can say at this point in time is that we're following up some leads. I understand the ME's office did contact you

118

with the results of the autopsy and released the body for burial?" I asked, addressing my question to Mrs. Tatum.

"They said she was suffocated," Mrs. Tatum said, dabbing her eyes with a spent Kleenex. "And yeah, we buried her. Them Marshalls even tried to come to the funeral. But I put a stop to that! I had my husband run 'em off."

"We've already spoken to the sheriff of Tejas County about an injunction to keep the Marshalls away from my client and her family."

I almost laughed. "And did Sheriff Williams oblige you?" I asked.

"He's looking into the situation," Ass said. "This is pursuant, of course, to the civil action we plan on bringing against them."

Looked like Ass Blakley had found himself some deep pockets, namely Dixon Marshall.

I stood up. "Miz Tatum, again, I'm sorry for your loss. From all accounts, your Amanda was a beautiful, sweet girl. We're doing the best we can here, following up every lead—"

Becca Tatum stood and poked a finger in my direction. "You find that Marshall boy! That Mr. Big Britches Trent! He's the one done this! Mark my word! He's hiding out, thinking his daddy's gonna make all this go away, his daddy with his big bucks! Well, I ain't letting this go! He kilt my little girl and he's gonna pay!"

"Ma'am, we have no proof that Trent Marshall was involved with your daughter's death. As of this point, we're not even sure Trent's still alive. Whoever killed Amanda may have killed Trent, too. We just don't know. As soon as we know anything, though, I'll get in touch with you."

Ass Blakeley pounded a business card onto my desktop. "Don't call my client, Sheriff. All communication is to go through me. I don't want you people bothering her."

"And I thought you came in here because we weren't bothering her enough," I said.

Blakeley put his hand on Becca Tatum's shoulder, moving her toward the door. "Call me," he demanded, then they were gone.

I sat back down in my swivel chair and thought about how much I disliked Ashton Simon Blakeley, and figured poor Becca Tatum deserved better than that.

I figured I didn't owe Laura and her husband diddly-squat, but I called Dixon Marshall's office anyway. I didn't call the home, not wanting to talk with Laura directly. My last conversation with her still rankled.

I got through to Marshall after only two secretaries. "Sheriff," he said. "What can I do for you?"

"I just got a visit from Becca Tatum, Amanda Nederwald's mother, and her lawyer," I said. "Just wanted to give you a heads-up."

"Sheriff Williams called us yesterday. Seems Mrs. Tatum wants to put a restraining order against Laura and me."

"That's what I hear. And possibly a civil action of some sort."

Marshall laughed. "I've known Ashton Blakeley for a while, Sheriff Kovak, and I must tell you I'm not quaking in my boots about that little shitheel."

I grinned in spite of myself. "Good thinking on your part, Mr. Marshall."

"Any word?" he asked, sobering.

"No, sir. Still tracking down leads. The investigation is still open, and we'll find the boy, one way or the other."

"By the 'other' I assume you mean dead?" he said.

"It's a possibility," I answered.

"Don't tell his mother that," he said.

120

"No, sir," I answered.

Marshall sighed. "It's not looking good, is it, Milt?"

"Don't give up hope yet," I said. "We just don't know enough."

"Please keep me posted," he said.

I agreed and hung up. Sometimes my job just wasn't much fun.

Later that afternoon, while I was doing dreaded paperwork, Gladys called to say my sister was on the line. I looked at the state forms on the statistical analysis of criminal behavior, broken down into type of crime committed, broken down by gender, age, race et cetera, and at the telephone, trying to decide which was worse.

I picked up the phone. "Hey, Jewel," I said.

"Hey yourself, big brother," she said, her voice pleasant for a change.

I relaxed. "What's up?"

"I just wanted to thank you for everything, Milt. Marlene's not the only one who needs to be expressing her gratitude to people. I don't know what I would have done without you that night," she said, sighing, both of us knowing which night she referred to. To my sister, I'm afraid, it will always be "that night."

"Hey, honey, it's family. No need—"

"If you can't thank your family, Milt, what good are the words to anyone else? I just want you to know I love you."

I sat there stunned, not knowing what to say. Finally, thinking what my wife Jean would do in this situation, I said, "I love you, too, little sister."

I heard a sob on the other end of the line. Then she laughed. "Wow, this is silly! Seriously grown people not knowing how to say those words to each other."

I laughed, embarrassed. "Yeah, I know. Hey, y'all wanna come to dinner Friday?" I asked, instantly regretting the spontaneous offer without having my wife's okay. This was going to get me a lecture on mutual respect if ever anything did.

"Check with Jean first," Jewel said, reading my mind.

I grinned to myself. "Yeah, I will. Then I'll call and extend the real invitation."

"I'll look forward to the possibility," she said, then gave me a quick good-bye.

I immediately called Jean and got her between patients. "How 'bout we invite Jewel and Harmon over for dinner Friday night?" I asked.

"You already have, haven't you?" Jean said.

"Well, sort of."

"Sort of?"

"I invited but Jewel wouldn't accept until you gave the okay."

"Which makes me the bad guy if I say no," my wife reasoned. "Honestly, Milt, sometimes I feel like you just don't think!"

"Honey, she said she loved me. What else could I do?"

Jean was silent a moment, then sighed and said, "Absolutely nothing. But you'll cook."

I decided not tell my sister that part of the plan when I called her back to confirm.

Wednesday I got a call from Bobbie Turnball, the cute little girl at Roy Higgins's office. "I got some e-mails from those people in the cult survivors group, Sheriff," she said. "If you give me your e-mail address I'll send them to you."

Well, she had me there. There was a computer sitting on my desk, and, as I understood it, it did have e-mail and Internet capabilities. I'd turned it on once, then hurriedly turned it off. That had been six months ago.

"My e-mail's down," I said, having heard that expression somewhere.

"Oh, okay, how 'bout I fax it to you?"

We had a fax machine, out by Gladys's desk, but I had no idea what the number was or how you used it.

"Ah, I need to go downtown anyway, Bobbie. How 'bout I just pop by your office and you show me?"

I could almost hear her grin on the other end of the line. "I'll print out the e-mails, Sheriff."

I sighed. "That'll be handy," I said, and hung up.

Bobbie was wearing jeans and a different T-shirt, this one orange and sporting a multicolored bejeweled butterfly. Her hair, bangs still straight across her forehead, was pulled back in a ponytail today. She'd progressed from twelve-year-old to fourteen-year-old.

"So how's that nephew, Sheriff?" she asked by way of greeting.

"Coming home for the weekend real soon," I said.

She stood up and came around her desk, a sheaf of papers in her hand. "Mr. Higgins is in court right now, not due back for a couple of hours. Feel free to use his office," she said, opening the door for me.

I thanked her and went in, picking the couch and coffee table. "You want something to drink?" Bobbie asked me.

"You got any soda pop?" I asked.

"There's a Coke machine out in the hall."

I handed her some change. "Coke sounds real good, a real one, not diet," I said, then settled down on the sofa.

The first e-mail was from Newbetter. "Talked to the group last night and explained your problem," it read. "One of the gals in the group, 'Shazam42,' knew Grigsby in Colorado.

Wants you to e-mail her for more details, but did say Grigsby was a real creep. Alma was Mrs. Grigsby by the time Shazam42 knew them, so she had no background on her. Said Grigsby's thing at that time was survival at the millennium. Wanted to start a whole new race when the world exploded. Only his group would survive. Had a setup somewhere in the mountains, with caves or something. But then, of course, the millennium came and nobody died, so he went out of business in Colorado. Had to move on—to your neck of the woods, it seems. Anyway, e-mail Shazam42 and she'll give you more detail. There was some other stuff but 473cultless will cover that. Let us know when you can what's going on so we can get it in our databank and posted on our Web. We're trying to DO SOMETHING about these assholes!"

Bobbie came in with a can of Coke and a glassful of ice. "What have you read so far?" she asked me.

"Newbetter's e-mail. Did you e-mail this Shazam42?" I asked her.

"Sure did, first thing. I'll check again in a little bit, see if she's answered."

"What did you ask her?" I asked.

"Just anything she knew about Grigsby or his wife. Or if she'd heard of the Seven Trumpets out here. Just general information."

I nodded.

"Read 473cultless's mail? It's interesting."

That was the next page. It read, "Dear Lawsweetie, I have a mental image of you—kind of hot in a short skirt like Ally McBeal. Am I close? Yes, I'm flirting, but then again, why not? You don't flirt, you don't get, right? Anyway, about this Alma Taggert. Seems she and Alma Smith are one and the same, according to my source in the group, guy named Bug. He got strung out with Taggert when he was like fourteen. Said she

124

liked to stroke little boys. Didn't get much beyond that—like I wanted to hear. TMI. The bitch . . ."

I looked at Bobbie. "TMI?" I asked.

"Too much information," she said.

"Oh," I said, and went back to reading.

"Anyway, Bug said she'd get up to five kids in the van, mostly boys but some girls, pray at 'em all day, save their souls, grope 'em all night. Yuck. Then she'd send them out selling flowers on street corners, you know, the usual, take the money, and feed them the usual cult slop—oatmeal, rice, mashed potatoes, anything low on protein and high on starch. When any of the kids got uppity, she'd notify a parent she'd 'found' their kid, ask for a reward, most always get it, and send the kid home. Then pick up another to replace that one. Bug said he saw the light the hard way. One of the girls Alma picked up was only twelve and Bug had a thing for her. They got to be tight, you know, as friends, nothing dirty. When Alma realized they were getting tight, she accused them of having sex, then she tried to make Bug cut the girl's hair. She had real long blond hair, he said. When he wouldn't do it, she shaved the girl's head, then called Bug's parents, said she 'found' him. When he left he tried to take the girl with him, but then Alma got physical with him, knocked him around. Pretty much cured the kid of wanting anything to do with cults. I tried to get him to talk to you direct, but he's real skittish. The kid's only seventeen, lurked in our room for a couple of months before he ever said anything. Couldn't get him to contact you. Sorry. I'll keep trying, though. And, by the way, about that short little lawyer skirt????"

I looked at Bobbie. "You did tell him you were spoken for by my nephew, right?"

"Totally," she said, grinning. "I explained my heart is under lock and key, to be opened only by someone named Leonard."

She looked at me. "When we're married, can I call him Lenny?"

I shrugged. "You might try it after the engagement is official, but watch your step."

"The next one is a second one from Newbetter. I've put them in chronological order, as they came in on my e-mail."

I nodded and grabbed the next page. "Lawsweetie—sorry to tie up your e-mail but I just heard from a member who wasn't online last night. Missed the meeting. But he heard about your question from one of the group and had some information concerning Alma Smith. This would be in Utah, from what I could gather between her NV time as Alma Taggert and her CO time as Alma Grigsby. I asked him to e-mail you directly and he said he would. If you don't hear from him by tomorrow, e-mail me and I'll get back to him. Don't like to give out members' e-mail addresses without permission. BTW, his tag's 'NB7SB6.' "

I looked at Bobbie. "BTW—by the way," she said. "His is the next e-mail."

The next one was from NB7SB6. "Lawsweetie. Newbetter gave me some 411 on your quest re: Alma Taggert/Smith/Grigsby. I knew her as Smith in Provo, Utah. She was purporting to be a direct descendent of Joseph Smith, the founder of the Church of the Latter-Day Saints—you know, Mormons. Which was crap. I don't think anybody bought that, but she had a good spiel and managed to get some Mormon wives involved. And their kids, of course. Ol' Alma definitely likes the kiddies. Didn't last long, though. Mormons are a suspicious lot—the men didn't like Alma a bit and when one kid said something about Sister Alma's 'touch therapy' sessions, the shit hit the fan. She got out of Provo minutes before the tar and feathering. Which, personally, I'd like to have seen. I was on the side of good by that time and have been trying to keep an eye out for crap floating to the top in the Utah area. Sister Alma floated up nice and bloated. I heard she headed for Colorado and got involved with some ex-con out there who was preaching millennium madness. Hope this helps."

That was the last of the e-mails. "What do you think?" Bobbie asked me.

"I think something stinks up at the Seven Trumpets," I said.

"Ha!" she said. "I knew it!" She jumped up from the couch. "Let me check my e-mail—see if we've heard from Shazam42."

She left the room, only to call out in less than a minute, "It's here!"

I went into the outer office and read over her shoulder. "Lawsweetie, got your name from Newbetter re: Grigsby. You've got yourself a real banana on your hands. From what I could find out after he left here (and yes, I was 'indoctrinated' by Brother Grigsby, but I'll get to that in a minute), Grigsby already had a record before I met him—he was jailed in some bubba state—"

"Hey," I said, "we're a bubba state!"

"And proud of it," Bobbie replied. "She's a Yankee, Sheriff, what do you expect?"

"True," I said, and we kept reading.

"—in some bubba state for fraud. Don't know if it was his usual cult scam or something else. Couldn't get any 411 on that. Records sealed for some reason—"

"But you could get that!" Bobbie said. "You know, being sheriff and all."

"Yeah, you're right. I could."

"Is your e-mail really down or do you just not know how to use it?" she asked.

I just looked at her. "Because if it's the second one," she said, "casting no aspersions, Sheriff, I could go over to your

127

office and help you access the right sites to get this information."

I sighed. "I turned it on—once," I said.

"They can be real intimidating," she said, rather condescendingly, I thought.

We went back to reading Shazam42's e-mail. "Records sealed for some reason—don't know why. His scam here was millennium-oriented. Convinced people—yours truly included—that the world would end, 12-31-99. For everybody who didn't know what to do, that is. He, of course, knew what to do. He had some land he'd gotten from some old geezer who thought Grigsby was God himself, and the land backed up to a mountain that had all sorts of caves winding through it. We were all going to hide out in these caves come the millennium and be the only people left on earth. Then we'd start our new race. Except for the old man who owned the property, Grigsby was the only male in the place. His idea was to start a whole new race with his sperm alone. And, yep, you guessed it, indoctrination consisted primarily of being jumped by the good brother. And strangely enough, good Sister Alma was usually in the room. Creepy, huh? As luck would have it, 12-31-99 came and went and the rest of the world was still here, and all us girls began asking questions. Then he decided to pick another date. Said everybody knew the real eve of the millennium was 12-31-00. By this time it was the third month since my first 'indoctrination' and I was still getting my periods. And I began to think maybe I was kind of lucky my 'indoctrinations' weren't working. Neither was anyone else's that I knew of then. I tiptoed out of the retreat in February, me and five other girls. That left twelve. By the time we got to Denver my toes were frostbit—lost two—and one of the girls lost a finger. And by then we were all good and mad. It's amazing what a couple of hamburgers

128

on the road—you know, all that PROTEIN—can do for your mind. We were ready to turn Grigsby's ass in by the time we reached Denver. But the cops wouldn't do anything. All the girls were overage, and he wasn't doing anything 'wrong,' well, at least not illegal. I've kept in touch with the five who escaped with me and thank God nobody got pregnant, but we don't know what happened to the other twelve. I heard Grigsby got shut down when the old geezer died and his kids wanted the land back. But what happened with those twelve girls, I don't know. If I give you a list of their names, can you find out if some of them ended up where you are? You mentioned Seven Trumpets in your e-mail. That's not surprising, Grigsby had a real thing for Revelations. Almost exclusively the text he preached from—and he preached to us three times a day. How did I get into this? I have no idea. It seems like another world—except when I look at my left foot. Please let me know if you'll look for the others and I'll e-mail you a list of names."

"Should I e-mail her back?" Bobbie asked.

"Oh, I really want that list of names," I said.

Bobbie got a clear screen to e-mail Shazam42 back. "Ask her for the list and anything else she can think of. Ask her if she's ever heard of Barry Leventhwart or a girl named Ruth— that's supposedly Barry's wife. Dark hair, pretty, brown eyes. Mole on her left cheek."

Bobbie typed all that in and hit "send." We'd have to wait, like, you know, hours, for an answer.

129

9

Bobbie sent her phones to the answering service, left a note for Roy, and went with me back to the station for my first real computer lesson.

The computer came right on, which surprised me since I hadn't turned it on for six months, but Bobbie said it wasn't like an old Chevy whose battery ran down from lack of use. I tried not to take the condescending remark personally, and decided I'd still introduce her to Leonard.

She showed me the "icon" on my "menu" that could get me to the Internet and then just clicked on it and, lo and behold, what seemed like only a few seconds later, we were in a "search engine."

"Since we don't have an address for what we're looking for, we'll just do a general search." She got up from the chair and told me to sit down. "You're going to do this," she said.

I just looked at her.

Bobbie grinned. "You can do it, Sheriff. I swear you can."

"Ever heard the expression—"

"Old dog, new tricks?" she suggested.

"I was thinking more about the one that says really good-looking men shouldn't bother their pretty heads with this kind of thing?"

"No, never heard that one." She lifted my hands to the keys. "Just like a typewriter, Sheriff. Now, type in 'Louisiana' and see if we can find any law enforcement sites mentioned."

I did what she asked, misspelling "Louisiana" the first time but getting it the second. Something came up saying there were like over a hundred thousand "hits."

I looked at Bobbie and by her expression back to me, I must have looked terrified. "That just means there are that many things on the Internet with the word 'Louisiana' mentioned. Now we narrow the search. Type in 'law enforcement.'"

She kept me at it until we came up with the Baton Rouge Police Department Web site address. Then she made me highlight that, click, and boom, we were there. My head was spinning but I was beginning to see where this computer thing could be a mite useful.

"You know, I coulda called on the telephone to Baton Rouge a lot quicker," I said, eager to be in what my wife would call "denial."

"And they probably would have referred you to a database." Bobbie leaned over me and punched some keys, then said, "What's your code?"

"Huh?" I said.

Bobbie sighed. "Your code. You don't know your code, of course. You didn't even know you had a code. Does anybody in this place ever use the computer?" she asked, getting a little irritated. I'd have to tell Leonard about this tendency, I thought.

"Gladys does some," I said.

"The lady out front?" she asked.

I nodded.

"Be right back," Bobbie said and ran out the door. In a minute I could hear her and Gladys laughing. Since Gladys didn't do a lot of that, I figured the laughter was at my expense.

Bobbie laid a slip of paper in front of me. "Type that in," she said.

I did. The computer screen did some kind of dance, and lo and behold, I was at a place that would actually let me ask a question.

"Type in Grigsby's name," Bobbie said.

I did and a new screen rolled up. "Theodore Davis Grigsby, aka Donald Clyde Malvin, d/o/b 8-24-58—"

Bobbie said, "Ha! I knew it! A Leo!"

". . . height 6'2", weight 165 lbs., brown/brown. Arrest record: 12-07-92, Baton Rouge, LA, unlawful use of funds/fraud—charges dropped; 10-14-89, Natchez, MS, child endangerment/kidnapping—charges dropped; 7-6-81, Dallas, TX, statutory rape—sentenced 5 yrs.—served 2, probation 3. Juvenile record Mineral Wells, TX, sealed."

"This is not a nice man," Bobbie said, reading over my shoulder.

"Why do so many Texas bad boys end up here?" I lamented.

"Maybe 'cause you're such a challenge?" Bobbie suggested, a twinkle in her eye.

Okay, I'd let her meet Leonard after all.

After promising Bobbie a rib-eye dinner with my nephew, my treat, I got Dalton to drive her back to her office and picked up my phone on the second ring. Gladys with the glad tidings that Laura Marshall was on line one.

"Miz Marshall," I said, picking up the phone.

"Milt," she said, her voice honey-sweet. "I just called to apologize. I had no right to talk to you the way I did."

132

I didn't say anything. It's an old cop trick—or I couldn't think of anything to say, one or the other.

"I really am sorry, Milt. I'm just so upset about Trent, I don't know what to do. Have you heard anything?"

"No, ma'am," I said. "Nothing new. Like I said before, we're tracking down some leads. Getting more information every day. I hope to know something shortly."

In other words, I got diddly-squat, ma'am.

"Well, I knew you'd call if you had anything to report. It's just that I hated leaving things the way we did the other day. You know I've always cared a great deal for you, Milt. I was just striking out—"

"Ma'am, I'll call you or your husband if anything comes up. But right now I got another call on the line—"

"Yes, of course. I'm sorry to keep you."

"Bye, Miz Marshall," I said and hung up.

The only thing worse than having Laura Johnson yelling accusations at me was having Laura Johnson being sweet. I wasn't up to handling either one.

I was packing up to leave my office when Gladys put another call through to me.

"Hey, Sheriff, it's me, Bobbie?" she said.

"Hey, Bobbie," I said. "What's up?"

"I got an answer to that e-mail we sent shazam42. Want me to transfer it to your e-mail?"

"It's got that list of names?"

"Yeah. I'm going to transfer it and Gladys can help you bring it up, okay?"

I sighed. "Okay, I guess."

"You can do it, Sheriff," Bobbie said, like talking a kid into his first solo bike ride. "I know you can!"

"Thanks," I said and hung up, calling Gladys back to my desk.

Gladys came in and sat down at the computer, pulling up my e-mail. "You've never checked this, huh?" she said. There seemed to be a lot of stuff on there.

"Well, no, not exactly," I said.

"Milt, Milt, Milt," she said, shaking her head. "There's probably stuff on here you shoulda read months ago."

"Just show me Bobbie's e-mail, okay, Gladys?"

She brought it up and left the room. I sat down and read. "Lawsweetie, the name you mentioned—Ruth—there was a girl at the compound here Grigsby called Ruth, who fits the description you sent. Her real name was Cara Carlisle. Real meek, just right for Grigsby. Never heard of Barry Leventhwart. If she's married to him had to be Grigsby's doing. Cara would do whatever Grigsby told her. I always thought the girl wasn't playing w/ a full deck, but I can't specify why. Just a feeling. Here's the list of the other girls I could remember. Checked with some of the ones got out with me and this is all we came up w/. I marked what names were Grigsby-given, and what names were real that I knew. Didn't know that many last names. Sorry. The only reason I knew Cara's last name was because she had "CCC" on her underwear and I asked—said it stood for 'Cara Carleen Carlisle.' Some parents just don't have much sense, do they? Anyway, anytime you need me, let me know. And please get back w/ us on what's going on so we can get it in the database. Thanks."

That was followed by a list of names:

Jude (g)
Mary (g) real name Laura
Peter Ann (g) real name Amy
Naomi (g) real name Jennifer Lawson

Katherine (g)

Ruth (g) Cara Carlisle

Esther (g) real name Christina (last named
started w/ a b)

Magdalene (g)

Maria (g) real name was also Maria—Hispanic
last name

Rebecca (g) real name Linda Reemer, from San
Diego, CA.

The list contained only ten names. In her earlier e-mail she
said when the six of them had left the Colorado retreat they'd
left twelve girls behind. I'd have to get Bobbie to follow up
on that.

I turned off the computer—all on my own—picked up my
briefcase, and headed home.

Friday came and I knew I wasn't up to cooking for the whole
herd of family coming my way. Plus, Leonard was coming
home for the weekend and I'd invited Bobbie Turnball over
for dinner. Then, of course, Jewel had called and said Marlene
wanted to bring Clifford, who was now a welcome member
of the family, and I wouldn't mind, would I? What could I
say? At noon I called the Longbranch Inn and ordered food
to pick up at five when I left the office. I figured I could handle
the warming-up part at home just fine.

It took two trips to carry in the tin-foil pans laden with
food, while my wife just crossed her arms and looked at me,
one eyebrow raised. "This is you cooking?" she finally said.

"Yep, if you want people to actually eat," I said, taking the
stuff into the kitchen. The only really good meal I could make
was beans and weenies. I chop a mean weenie. But somehow,
this occasion seemed to call for more than that. After all, my

135

sister had said she loved me. Can you celebrate that with beans and weenies? I don't think so.

Jean watched while I got out the good china and silver and crystal and set the dining room table, using cloth napkins and the good napkin rings and everything. It looked real nice when I got finished. Then Jean came in with some flowers from the backyard. She got out her good crystal vase and arranged the flowers, putting them in the center of the table. "The pièce de résistance," she said. We smiled at each other.

Then I got out the good serving bowls, warmed up the food in the tin foil-pans on the stove top, and was ready for the herd.

They didn't disappoint. They came in two cars, Jewel and Harmon in one car, Marlene, Leonard and Carl in Clifford's red Mustang, Clifford behind the wheel.

Johnny Mac hadn't had a chance to see his cousin Leonard "that night," he greeted him delightedly. Leonard has a way with kids—I just hoped that way would work with Bobbie Turnball.

She showed up ten minutes after the others. When she rang the bell, I answered, being the only one who knew her, and ushered her in. Her hair was down, a lustrous brown, curling at the ends, the bangs still straight across. She'd dressed up for the occasion, a short, straight denim skirt and a blue T-shirt from a Garth Brooks concert.

Jean warmed to her immediately, as did my sister, and the younger kids thought she was great. Bobbie and Leonard took one look at each other and it was instant dislike.

I decided I was definitely out of the matchmaking business.

Dinner, however, was a success. I served pot roast with new potatoes and baby carrots, sides of green beans with pearl onions, corn on the cob, and coleslaw, with apple pie for dessert. Everyone told Jean how great the meal was.

"Don't thank me," she said, resting her pert little chin on her palm, as she stared at me across the table. "Milt was responsible for dinner."

A hush fell over the room. My sister looked at me, looked at the food, then said, "You got this at the Longbranch Inn, didn't you?"

"You'da preferred beans and weenies?" I asked.

Jewel laughed and Marlene changed the subject. "So what's going on with the investigation, Uncle Milt?"

"Nothing new as far as finding the boy," I said, "but we are finding out a lot about the good Brother Grigsby."

"Like he's got a record as a long as your arm!" Bobbie said.

I shot her a look. "Confidential information, Miss-I-Work-for-a-Lawyer-and-Should-Know-Better," I said.

"Oops," she said. "Sorry. I just thought since you shared the information with me, it was okay."

"What kind of record?" Marlene asked, leaning forward, eager for the information.

I'd shared with her before and felt it had brought us closer. And besides, this was family.

"Yeah, with Bobbie's help, I was able to track down a lot of information about both Brother Grigsby and his wife. Neither one of them are sweetness and light, let me tell you. She's escaped prosecution by the skin of her nose several times, and he's actually been arrested a lot—though he only served once, a two-year stint. Shoulda been in there longer, but got out for good behavior."

"What did they get him for?" Marlene asked.

"Statutory rape!" Bobbie answered.

Now I had almost decided not to mention that, but there it was, out in the open. I shot Bobbie another look.

"If you want me to shut up, Sheriff, just say so!" she said, shooting me her own look.

"How old was he at the time?" Leonard asked.

I did some mental figuring. "About twenty-five, thereabouts," I said.

"Then statutory rape means nothing," Leonard said. "Depending on the state, the girl could have been as old as twenty." Looking at his little brother, Leonard explained, "Statutory rape just means that a guy over twenty-one had sex with a girl under twenty-one."

"Or under eighteen, in some states," I said.

"Is this proper dinner-table conversation?" Jewel interjected. She was universally ignored.

"Sure, a seventeen-year-old girl comes on to some poor twenty-two-year old schmuck and *he* ends up in prison!" Leonard said.

"And who're you to say at what age a girl is old enough to consent? Seventeen? Fourteen? Twelve?" Bobbie shot back.

"All I'm saying," Leonard said, to the room at large, not to Bobbie, "is the guy was only twenty-five. Now if he was thirty-two and the girl was seventeen, maybe we'd be talking about something!"

"Numbers!" Bobbie said. "All you guys think about is facts! What about feelings? Huh? A seventeen-year-old can be just as immature as a fourteen-year-old and be just as traumatized by sex with a twenty-five-year-old! Don't give me numbers!"

Leonard turned red but didn't say anything. Jean broke the silence. "Bobbie has a point. But the main point is, we don't know the circumstances of this particular arrest and conviction. But from what Milt has said, Leonard, I think you might be defending the wrong man."

"I'm not defending him!" Leonard said, his face still red. "I'm just saying—"

"That men can do whatever they want and women just have to put up with it?" Bobbie suggested sweetly.

Leonard finally turned and looked at her. "No, I didn't say that, but you knee-jerk femi-Nazis like to take *anything* a man says and twist it to your own end!"

"Femi-Nazi?" Bobbie hooted.

"What's a femi-Nazi?" Carl asked, at the same time that Jewel said, "This was certainly a delicious meal, Milt."

"Who's for dessert?" I asked.

Except for my matchmaking disaster, the evening was a success.

As I walked Bobbie to her car, I asked her if she'd heard back from Shazam42. "She said that's all they could remember. She might have said wrong when she said there were twelve girls still there when the six of them left."

"Are all six still accounted for?" I asked her.

"According to Shazam42, yeah. She still talks to all of 'em. They're scattered, she said. A couple like her still in Colorado, one in Seattle, one in California, and one on the East Coast. They e-mail. All of them are still very much into getting Grigsby, so they'll give us any help we need."

I decided to ignore the "us." That's all I needed, a nineteen-year-old femi-Nazi deputy. Whatever a femi-Nazi was.

"Look, Bobbie, I want to thank you a lot for all your help—"

"Whoa, now, Sheriff. Just because your nephew and I decided not to get married right away, that doesn't mean you're ditching me, too, does it?"

I laughed awkwardly. "Course not, Bobbie. Tell you what, I'd be real grateful if you'd keep on the computer end of things. You know I'm not good at that. Keep in contact with Shazam42 and the others, see what you can find out. You know—"

"Yeah, I know. Busy work." She sighed. "Well, Sheriff, it was fun." She tiptoed up to kiss me on the cheek. "You're cuter than your nephew. Too bad you're taken." Then she was off.

And I was "aw-shucksing" it all over the place. Women. Go figure.

After Bobbie left, Jewel and Jean took Johnny Mac upstairs to the playroom while Leonard, Carl and Clifford went out to look at Clifford's car engine. Marlene, as a female, wasn't particularly interested, so she and I stayed in the living room with Harmon.

"So what do you think has happened to the boy, Amanda's boyfriend?" Marlene asked.

I shook my head. "Honey, I just don't know. I'm praying he's alive, but if he is, then I gotta think he had something to do with the girl's death." Again I shook my head. "But with what all I'm finding out about Grigsby, I gotta think he's got a hand in it somewhere, too, although his record hasn't hinted at any violence."

I told her what we had learned on the Internet, going into more detail than I had at dinner. I was beginning to think my little niece was going to follow in my footsteps. She'd finish high school in another year, maybe go on to college, then enter the Academy . . .

"You know," Marlene said, "I'm pretty good on the computer. Maybe I could help Bobbie."

"I don't want anything interfering with your schoolwork," I started.

"I'm talking after school, of course, Uncle Milt. I can e-mail Bobbie, see what I can help her with."

I shrugged. "Sounds good to me, honey. I'd appreciate the help."

We beamed at each other while Harmon picked up an old copy of the *Longbranch Gazette* and ignored us.

I took the weekend off. Our weekend dispatcher had orders to call me at home if anything came up with the Seven Trumpets case, but the phone was pleasantly silent, at least no calls from the department.

Saturday Jean and Johnny Mac and I went antique shopping, which is one of Jean's true joys. Jean's more of a purebred when it comes to antiques—she likes to travel through the little towns hitting junk shops, seeing if she can find a treasure among all the trash. Once she'd found a small Waterford crystal vase in a boxful of mason jars and tea goblets. And then there was the time she found a clock by some famous German clock maker stuck in a drawer of an old beat-up fifties dresser. We bought the dresser without telling the owner about the clock. I'm not sure if that was exactly nice, but Jean said in the antique biz, anything goes.

That Saturday wasn't so productive. She found an album case for a set of 78-rpm records of Carmen Miranda, but no records were inside. She dickered the dealer down to a dollar for the case and came away smiling. We spent what I considered way too much on a turn-of-the-century penny bank for Johnny Mac (not that he'd be able to touch the darn thing until he was an adult). It was one of those mechanical things where you put the penny in the hand of an organ grinder's monkey and he'd walk two steps and put the penny in the organ grinder's cup, which was actually the penny bank. Johnny Mac and I had deposited a good twenty or so pennies before Jean said it was time to retire the bank to a top shelf of Johnny Mac's room. For looking at only, she told him.

Sunday was a perfect day—sunny and bright, the temperature hovering around seventy-five most of the day. It was my turn and the three of us went to the Baptist Church in Longbranch. We take turns—one Sunday the Baptist Church, the next the Catholic Church. Jean and I decided we wanted to

141

let Johnny Mac make up his own mind, so we had him baptized as a Catholic as an infant, and planned on letting him get dipped when he was twelve by the Baptists. Going back and forth, though, I had this horrible feeling one day Johnny Mac would end up in the Catholic confessional for his Baptist sin of having danced the night before.

Religion is a tricky business.

We spent the rest of Sunday playing and working in the yard, just doing things old married people with little kids do. It was nigh onto a perfect day.

Monday dawned wet and mean. The sky was black, heavy with lightning and thunder, with intermittent showers, as the weatherman is wont to say. It was my week to drive Johnny Mac to day care, which had me running a little behind as I got to the office. Which is why I walked in on the mess instead of having been there when it started.

"How dare you imply that my daughter would do anything of the sort!" Councilwoman Aleeta Haines was saying. She's a big woman, not fat but big. Must be six feet in her stocking feet and probably ran over two hundred pounds. Most of it, I'd say, was pure-dee muscle.

Her daughter stood next to her, and Lordy, that girl could *stand*. Like her mama, the younger Haines was tall, but all the muscle seemed to be massed around the chest. The girl did have some, as that guy in that movie once said, "bodacious ta-tas." She had lots of flaming-red hair, not exactly a natural-looking color, and was dressed in very tight, very short cut-off jeans and a halter top that was trying real hard to corral those larger-than-necessary breasts.

Jasmine Bodine was facing the two—at least I finally figured out it was Jasmine Bodine. The creature I beheld had platinum-blond hair—*big* hair—so much makeup on it was hard to see an actual face, and was wearing a skimpy little black leather miniskirt, a spangly red halter top, and spike heels that almost toppled her over on her face.

"Jasmine," I said, coming up to the group, "what's going on?"

"She's one of 'em, Milt!" Jasmine said, pointing at the Haines girl. "I actually heard her making a date for money!"

"How dare you!" Councilwoman Haines shouted. "You are accusing my child of . . . of . . . my God! I can't even say it!"

"Prostitution!" Jasmine supplied for her.

Councilwoman Peevey slapped Jasmine in the face.

I got in there quick, grabbing Mrs. Haines's hand and pushing a righteously angry Jasmine away with my other hand.

"Now, hold on. Councilwoman, I don't want to be arresting you for assaulting an officer," I said.

"But she did!" Jasmine yelled. "She assaulted me and you saw it, Milt! So did Gladys, didn't you?"

Gladys piped in, "I sure did! Didn't I tell you this would happen if we got a Republican mayor?"

"Everybody calm down!" I shouted. Voices stopped and everyone looked at me. "Now, Miz Haines, I know you didn't mean to slap my deputy here, so if you apologize—"

"For what?" she screamed. "Protecting my child's reputation? No way am I apologizing to this sleazy woman—"

So, of course, Jasmine went for Miz Haines. While I was breaking this one up, I couldn't help but notice the Haines girl smiling slightly at the ruckus she'd caused.

Dalton came in and I gave Jasmine to him, holding on to Mrs. Haines's arm myself. Addressing the girl, I said, "And what have you got to say for yourself, young lady?"

She shrugged. "Not a fuckin' thing," she said.

"Melanie!" her mother yelled, stunned. "You do not talk like that!"

Melanie laughed. "Sorry, Mom. You're wrong. I do talk like that. You wanna hear some more?"

143

"That's it," I said. I let go of Mrs. Haines and took her daughter's arm instead. "You and me, young lady. The interrogation room."

"Ooh, big bad Milty gonna get rough with me? Honey, I like it rough—"

"Melanie!" her mother cried.

"Dalton, take Miz Haines back to my office and stay with her. Jasmine, go clean yourself up."

Leaving the rest, I escorted Melanie Haines back to the interrogation room, which also served as a meeting room, dining room, and any other kind of room we needed it to be.

The girl sat down in a chair, her body lazy, her legs stuck out in front of her, knees parted, in what I guess she thought was a sexy pose. I could've told her it wasn't.

"So you been turning tricks out at the Dew Drop?" I said, keeping my voice conversational.

"Bullshit," she said, bored with the subject.

"You're not turning tricks?"

"Only in Sunday school," she said, grinned at me, then ran her tongue lazily across her lips.

"You wanna give me a straight answer?" I said.

"How about some head instead?" she said. "I bet that gimp wife of yours can't get on her knees much, huh?" she said, sliding off the chair into a kneeling position.

I got up and grabbed her, throwing her back into the chair. "Cut it out, Melanie," I said.

She laughed. "You *do* like it rough, don't you, Milty?"

"How old are you?" I demanded.

"Old enough," she said, the grin still in place.

"You got any ID? I need to know whether to charge you as a minor or an adult."

The grin never faded. "You're not going to charge me with

anything, Sheriff," she purred. "Mama wouldn't like that. And Mama pays your bills."

I grinned back. "No, honey, she don't," I said. "This is the county. Now your mama may pay the police chief's bills, but the county commissioners pay my bills. Your mama don't work for the county, now does she, honey?"

The grin slipped off her face. She sat up and glared at me. "You can't charge me with shit! That stupid deputy of yours doesn't know what she's talking about! I was talking to my boyfriend!"

"You usually charge your boyfriend?"

Melanie sighed. "Tell my mother to get me a lawyer, please. And now I don't say another word." She crossed her arms over her chest and pressed her lips together.

Which was her best pose yet.

10

I had to send Jasmine home. She was my night deputy anyway, and this was the daytime, so she should be home resting. Somehow I didn't think she'd get much sleep. She was madder than a wet hen when I finally got her out of the shop and into the parking lot.

"You need to charge that woman, Milt!" she said, for what seemed the hundredth time. "She slapped me!"

"Now, normally, hon, I would," I said, trying to placate a wet hen, which just about anybody could tell you is a real hard thing to do. "But seeing as how this lady has some real clout in this town, and seeing as how you up and called her daughter a prostitute—"

"But, Milt, she is!"

"Well, yeah, I know, but you gotta see where that would come as a bit of a shock to a mama, now don't you see that, Jasmine?"

"She slapped me!"

"True, true," I agreed, patting her on her shoulder, which was now, thank God, covered in a chambray work shirt over jeans. "But we gotta consider the circumstances, hon."

146

Jasmine stopped in her tracks and turned and looked hard at me. "Milt, you call me 'hon' one more time and I'm liable to slap you."

I sighed. She was right, I was heading straight toward sexual harassment, or something or other. "Sorry," I said, getting real tired of this game. "But, Jasmine, you gotta calm down. This was a big case and you did real good. I'm proud of you. Now don't blow the whole thing over her slapping you."

"But—"

"I'm serious, Jasmine," I said, trying to look stern.

"But—"

"Go on home now," I said, patting her on the shoulder again. "Sleep on it. If you still wanna cause a ruckus about this when you come on duty tonight, then we'll talk. Right now, get some rest. You did good, Jasmine. Now sleep on it."

I didn't wait for another "but"; instead, I turned and headed back into the building. A minute later I heard Jasmine's old jalopy start up and heard tires squealing in the parking lot. I hoped she didn't get a ticket getting home, knowing that would just add fuel to an already pretty bright fire.

What I wanted to do was go back up to Seven Trumpets and have a real look around, but I knew I needed a search warrant to do that. So I called Judge Rodgers who's sort of known as sheriff-department-friendly, and explained the problem.

"So what would you be looking for, Sheriff?" he asked me.

"Any evidence of those two kids having been there, Your Honor," I said. "There's got to be something. I'm sorta stymied here, Your Honor. I surely do need some help."

"Well," Judge Rodgers said, pausing to think a minute. Finally, he said, "I can get you a limited warrant, Sheriff. To search the premises. What they got out there?"

I described the layout: the sanctuary building with the

kitchen and dining room, the two dormitory-style tents, and the two trailers.

"The two trailers: those are residences?"

"Yes, sir," I said.

"Then they gotta be off the warrant. I can get you the sanctuary building and the two tents. Maybe the vehicles. You want the vehicles?"

"Yes, sir. And the grounds."

"Grounds are okay. But records and the two residences are off-limits, Sheriff."

"Thank you, Your Honor."

"I'll get my clerk to draw it up. Come by in an hour."

"Yes, sir," I said. "Thank you—" I started again, but he was already off the line.

I mentally did a little jig and called up Emmett and Dalton for backup. We were gonna have some fun now.

Let me just say that my ex-nephew-in-law Barry wasn't happy. We showed up in force—which was me and Emmett and Dalton, but in this small a county, that's all the force we got—waving the warrant and honking the horns of the three units we brought. Coming together in one unit would've looked small-time, so we brought three. Intimidation can sometimes be a thing of beauty.

Barry didn't come out to the gate; instead, a guy I'd never seen before came out. He was real big, sumo-wrestler big, and looked pretty damned silly in those white homespun pajamas.

"What?" he said, which somehow seemed might be the whole of his vocabulary.

"We got a warrant," I said, waving same in the air. "Let us in now or we'll arrest you."

Sumo-boy must not have believed me; he turned tail and walked back up the dirt road whence he came. Dalton looked

148

at me. "Want me to jump the fence and get him?" he asked me.

Now, big as Dalton was, he was just a pimple on sumo-boy's butt, and I didn't feel like having an all-out altercation. "Let's just wait," I said. "Maybe he's going to get someone else."

It may not often be the case, but this time I was right. Five minutes later Barry came riding his bicycle down the dirt road. He braked to a stop and slid off, staring at me like I was a turd in a punch bowl.

"What now?" he asked.

I waved the warrant. "Gotta warrant to search the grounds, the sanctuary, the tents, and the vehicles. Signed, sealed, and delivered by Judge Rodgers. You wanna look?"

I handed the warrant over the gate and Barry grabbed it, read it quickly, then handed it back. "Milt, it's a wonder somebody hasn't killed you in your sleep," he said.

"Is that a threat, Barry?" I asked. I looked at Emmett and Dalton.

"Sure sounded like a threat, Sheriff," Emmett said, and Dalton nodded. "Think we should arrest him right now? Threatening a peace officer?"

Barry unlocked the gate and took down the road barbs so we could drive through. "It wasn't a threat," he said, "just an observation."

He got back on his bike and headed back up the dirt road; we passed him in our vehicles, leaving a cloud of dust hopefully for him to choke on.

I took the sanctuary building, Emmett the men's dorm and Dalton the women's.

The sanctuary itself was basically empty. There were those hard benches with no backs, a handmade pulpit with no shelves or drawers, and that was about it. Behind the pulpit was a bench that had hymnals stacked on it, but other than that, the place was bare.

Behind the sanctuary were the kitchen and dining hall. As we were between meals, the dining hall was pretty much empty, too. Several long folding tables were arranged in rows in the big room, chairs sitting upside down on top of the tables, more stacked along the walls, one on top of the other. The kitchen consisted of a long, cafeteria-style feeding line, behind which was the cooking area itself. I found one small bag of green beans; other than that, the foodstuff consisted of big bags of rice, macaroni, potatoes, and oatmeal, along with a small bag of sugar and a large bag of wheat flour. Like one of the guys online had said—lots of starch and no protein.

Besides the foodstuff, the shelves were full of utensils, pots, pans, serving dishes, and piles of plastic divided dishes, but nothing terribly interesting.

Next to the kitchen was a small room decked out as an office. As this was part of the sanctuary building, I deemed it appropriate to search. The warrant said "no records," so I'd have to walk a careful line in here.

The office appeared to belong to Sister Alma, what with her name scattered around here and there. There was a desk with an old Apple computer sitting on top, a desk chair, a credenza with the matching Apple printer, a small window, and a filing cabinet with a fax machine. I made myself believe I shouldn't touch the filing cabinet, much as I wanted to. The desktop had a scattering of papers, and I figured as long as I didn't move them around I wasn't exactly "searching records." What I saw appeared to be receipts for food deliveries, invoices for this and that: one for four cases of napkins, four cases of toilet paper, and four cases of paper towels; another invoice for a gross of soy seeds, two gross of potato plugs, and one gross of assorted vegetable seeds, and an invoice for medical supplies, including breast pumps, forceps, and a vacuum extractor.

Looked like the Seven Trumpets was getting ready for some deliveries. I wondered who would actually be assisting the women when they gave birth. Maybe they had a midwife in the group. Seemed likely. Could be ol' Alma her own self. That would be handy.

The drawers of the desk contained the usual office supplies, a few personal items, like tampons and hand lotion, and some stuff I didn't think someone who'd given up all worldly goods—like those at this retreat supposedly had—would need (like fingernail polish, lipstick, and an expensive-looking gold compact). One drawer was full of files and I figured that was off-limits, but I did glance at the little labels on each file, without actually touching anything. From the labels, they seemed to be innocent enough: receipts, invoices, taxes, inventory, etcetera.

The credenza held larger office supplies, like reams of paper for the computer printer, manila folders, hanging folders, just stuff like that. This could've been any office in any business in Prophesy County.

That was all there was to the sanctuary building, so I left and headed toward the dormitory tents, glancing as I went at the bigger trailer with the large cross on top. This was surely the residence trailer of Brother Grigsby and Sister Alma, and I would surely like a peek inside, but that was definitely off the warrant. As was the smaller trailer, the little silver Airstream, that housed Barry and his wife Ruth. Who I now knew was really the former Cara Carlisle. I couldn't help wondering whose baby that was she was carrying—her husband's or their fearless leader's.

Emmett was still inside the men's tent, and he was doing a thorough job. Not liking these people much probably had a little to do with the fact that he was tearing off all the bed-clothes, upending every mattress, and taking out all the contents of the little high-school-looking lockers against one wall. As far as the lockers went, there wasn't all that much to take out: a few toiletries, a change of white homespun pajamas, and what looked like their winter shoes—heavy rubber galoshes. Each locker appeared to house the exact same articles. No individuality here.

I left Emmett and went to the other tent. The tent Emmett had been in housed fifty cots and fifty lockers, and it looked like only about half of those were used. In the women's tent, there were more like sixty cots and as many lockers, and it seemed every one was in full use. Like I'd noticed before, there were a lot more women at the Seven Trumpets than men.

Like in most things, Dalton wasn't as thorough or as aggressive as Emmett. He'd been looking through the lockers, but not taking anything out, feeling the beds, but not removing the bedclothes or mattresses. I suggested he do what Emmett had done.

"Gosh, Milt, that's kinda mean. These ladies didn't do nothing," he said.

"We don't know that, Dalton. We're looking for any sign of the dead girl, and we gotta be thorough."

I went to one of the lockers and started taking everything out. He followed suit with another locker. It took an hour to go through the whole place.

After that we hit the grounds, dividing up and walking the whole retreat. It was pretty easy to tell what belonged to the retreat, as the whole thing was fenced off. I couldn't help wondering who had paid for that expensive-looking fence. I doubted it was Brother Grigsby.

On the west side the land went as far as the Cullum River, where a small dock reached out into the water, with a kayak sitting upside down on the dock. A rowboat was tied up to it on one side and a small motorboat with fishing gear on the other. I wondered if maybe Grigsby and Alma got to eat the occasional fish, while the rest of the group consumed nothing but starch.

On the south the land reached to the road where we'd come in, on the east to a mound of rocks and natural hill formations, and on the north to a utility road used by the next county. All told it was about a hundred acres and it took a while to walk the whole thing.

And we found a great big nothing.

The vehicles consisted of an old yellow school bus, a beat-up Honda Civic of a certain age, and about twelve bicycles. The school bus was clean—not a speck of dust or dirt, like somebody had recently swept it out. So was the Honda Civic. Clean as a whistle. Too clean, I thought.

It wasn't until we got into our three squad cars heading back to Longbranch that it dawned on me what we *hadn't* found.

I'd barely walked in the door to my house when the phone rang. "I got it," I yelled to Jean, who was in the kitchen getting supper ready.

I picked up the phone and said, "Kovak."

"Milt, it's Jasmine."

"Hey, Jasmine," I said, wincing.

"I got a ticket from the city cops!"

I sighed. "Well, you were going a little fast when you left the office," I said.

"I didn't get it leaving the office, Milt," she said, "I got it coming in just now. And it wasn't for speeding."

"What was it for?" I asked.

"A busted taillight," she said.

"Well—"

"Did you see me leave this morning, Milt?"

"Yeah—"

"Did I have a busted taillight?"

"Uh—"

"I just had new brake lights put on a month ago, Milt. There was nothing wrong with my taillights. But when I got out of the car to look, one was surely broken."

"Well—"

"And Andy Dample was standing there by the back of my car, his nightstick in his hand, Milt, and there was glass on the ground!"

It dawned on me I hadn't heard Jasmine's Eeyore voice in quite a while. The whine seemed to be replaced by righteous anger.

"You accusing Andy Dample of knocking out your tail-light?"

"You bet your ass I am! How long do you think it took that Haines bitch to get the chief to start harassing me?" she said.

I wanted to protest. But somehow I just couldn't. When Emmett was police chief of Longbranch, this would have been unheard of. But Emmett got fired, and his replacement was a butt-kissing asshole who I could see telling somebody like Andy Dample to make life hard on one of my deputies for the audacity of making life hard on a member of the city council.

"Did you pick up some of the glass?" I asked.

"When I tried, Andy threw me up against my car and started searching me. Like a criminal! But I did manage to kick some shards under my car. I got 'em after he left."

"Good. Put 'em in an evidence bag and mark 'em."

"Already did," Jasmine said, a smile in her voice.

"You lock the bag in the evidence room?"

154

"Yes, sir, witnessed and signed off on by Gladys and Dalton."

I smiled. "Very good," I said. "You get on duty. You get any grief from city, you call me ASAP."

"Yes, sir. And what are you gonna do?"

"I'm gonna call the chief," I said and hung up.

The chief of police of Longbranch, Larry Joe January, wasn't at his office, and when I called his home number, all I got was his machine. I decided not to leave a message at either place—I didn't want him ready for me. I thought the next morning would do. I'd approach the lion in his den, so to speak.

Jean called me to dinner and I rounded up Johnny Mac, who was on the floor in the kitchen making noises with trucks, and we sat down to dinner. Jean's a pretty good cook; unfortunately, she believes what they say about things like high cholesterol and too much sodium, and other such nonsense, so her cooking was a little on the good-for-you side. But mostly tasty, just the same. Though I did miss mashed potatoes and gravy, chicken-fried anything, and bacon. Lord, did I miss bacon. This night we had chicken stir-fry with Chinese noodles and vegetables and a side of fresh fruit. Like I said, tasty, but hardly filling.

After we got Johnny Mac off to bed, I got a beer and sat down in the living room with my lady.

"Got a question," I said to her.

"What's that?" she asked.

"You got lockers where a bunch of women live, right?"

"Okay," she said.

"In the lockers you find deodorant, panties, an extra pair of those white PJs, and a hairbrush or two. What's missing?"

"You mean besides the usual: makeup, hair spray, perfume, all that stuff?"

155

"Well, that they woulda given up, right?"

"Yeah. I guess."

"So what's missing?"

Jean looked thoughtful for a minute. Finally she said, "You got me. What's missing?"

Jean had had a hysterectomy when Johnny Mac was born, which is probably why she hadn't thought about it. But I'd lived with a mother, a sister, a first wife, and then my sister and her daughter for long enough to know what was missing.

"Sanitary stuff," I said. "Kotex, tampons, anything like that."

"Hum," Jean said.

"I know some of 'em are pregnant, but are they all?"

"There was nothing like that?"

"The only place I saw anything was a box of tampons in Sister Alma's desk. That's it."

"Enough for the whole group?" she asked.

I shook my head. "Small box," I said. "One of those ten-sized ones, I think."

"They're all pregnant," Jean said, awe in her voice.

"All of 'em?" I asked, incredulous.

"What else?"

"You think Brother Grigsby's been a real busy boy?" I asked.

"Milt, he's building his own world out there, all with his own seed."

"Adam and a bunch of Eves," I said.

11

When I got to the office next morning, there were three messages from Laura Marshall and two from her husband. I opted to call Mr. Marshall.

"Something up?" I asked.

"We heard from Trent," Dixon Marshall said immediately.

Oh, Jesus, I thought. The boy's alive. That meant he probably killed Amanda.

"When?" I asked.

"Last night, or this morning rather. Around three A.M."

"What did he say? Where is he?"

"He couldn't tell us. All he said was he was in trouble. He said he needed help. And, Sheriff, he asked us where Amanda was!"

"What did you tell him?"

"Nothing. We didn't have a chance. The phone went dead."

"Tell me exactly, word-for-word, what happened," I said.

Dixon Marshall took a deep breath. "The phone rang. It's on my side of the bed, so I picked it up. I said hello. Then I hear Trent's voice. I knew it was him immediately. He said, 'Dad, I'm in trouble!' Real rushed like. Then he said, 'You've

157

gotta help me! Where's Amanda, Dad?' I said, 'Trent, where are you?' And then the phone went dead. He coulda said something else, but by this time Laura was screaming and trying to grab the phone from me—"

"She's left several messages here, Mr. Marshall. I need you to call her and tell her we talked."

"Whatever," he said, his voice sounding exasperated. "What are you going to do about this?"

"You got caller ID?"

"Yes, but it was blocked. Either it was long distance or a cell phone."

"Okay, look. I'll call Bill Williams and have him get somebody out to your house to put a trace on the phones, okay? In case he calls again."

"Right," he said.

"Meanwhile, I want you to think real hard. Did you hear anything in the background? Any noises at all? Any way to identify where he was?"

"No, nothing. It was quiet. Echo-y sounding. Like he was in a cave or something. God, Milt, what does this mean? Where in the hell can he be?"

"Mr. Marshall, I need you to remain calm. You're gonna have to be the strong one here. His mother's gonna need you to be strong. And so is Trent."

Dixon Marshall sighed. "I know, I know. But I feel so useless. I need to do something, Milt! Anything! Tell me what to do."

"The only thing you can do right now, Mr. Marshall, is wait. I know that's hell, but that's all there is to it. I'm calling Bill Williams right now and we'll get somebody over to the house. This is your office number I called, right?"

Again he sighed. "Yes. I couldn't stand being in the house

with Laura and the kids. Laura was screaming and the kids were crying—"

"Well, Mr. Marshall," I said, "that's your job right now. Your only job. Taking care of your family. You need to go home and do that. I'll have somebody from Bill Williams's office over there as quick as I can."

"Yeah. You're right. I just never could bear to hear a woman cry. Really grates on my nerves."

"Gotta buck up, Mr. Marshall," I said.

"Yeah, you're right," he said and hung up.

Better him than me, I thought.

I called Bill Williams, sheriff of Tejas County, and explained the situation. He said he had a contact at the local telephone office and would get him and a deputy over to the Marshall's house straightaway.

After that I hung up and thought. Now what? The kid was alive. He asked after Amanda. Did that mean he didn't know Amanda was dead? Or was he trying to throw his stepfather off his track? Or did Marshall make that part up? It would be just like Laura to make up something like that, but I wasn't sure about her husband. He seemed like a straight arrow. But how straight an arrow could he be after being married to Laura Johnson for the past however many years?

Or maybe it was just me she corrupted. Maybe I wasn't giving Dixon Marshall his due. Maybe he could resist Laura's ways.

Or maybe he couldn't. After all, he married her, didn't he?

I got my mind off that train of thought. I needed to concentrate on the boy, not his mother. Whether or not Trent knew Amanda was dead or alive wasn't the point. The point was: Trent was alive, and he was in trouble. And I had one thing I needed to do: Find him and do it pretty damn quick.

The next phone call was from an irate female, all right, but not Laura Marshall. It was Jasmine.

"Have you talked to the chief yet, Milt?"

"I'm on my way over there now, Jasmine," I said.

"Well, you can tell him for me—"

"I'll do the talking, Jasmine. You get some sleep, okay?"

"They stopped me on my way home this morning," she said. "A warning this time. It was Troy Douglas. We went to high school together and I don't think he wants to play this game like Andy does. Anyway, he gave me a warning about a broken taillight. I told him Andy broke the damn taillight, but he didn't say anything. Just said to get it fixed and left."

"Jasmine, don't tell anybody else, especially on the police force, that Andy broke that light, okay?"

"Why the hell not?" she yelled. "He did!"

"We're gonna play this by the book, Jasmine. We got evidence, and if we have to we'll take it to a judge."

"And get all those fuckers locked up!" Jasmine said.

I'd never heard her say the F-word before and it took me aback. "Jasmine," I said, shocked.

"Well, Milt! I'm mad! I've got a right to be mad! And I'll say fuck if I want to. Fuck! Fuck! Fuck!"

I sighed. "Okay, Jasmine, whatever. You get some sleep. I'm on my way to the chief's office now."

"Give him hell, Milt!"

I rang off.

The police department was housed in the old courthouse on the town square in Longbranch. The sheriff's department used to be housed there too, but it was moved to the "new building," where we are now, out on the highway right outside the city limits, back in the sixties.

160

The police department was on the ground floor and I knew it intimately. Not only had my next-in-command Emmett Hopkins been chief of police there for many years, but I'd broken into the place myself a while back, right after Emmett had been booted out, to get the goods on the new chief of police Larry Joe January. Let's just say me and Larry Joe weren't the best of friends.

I asked at the counter for an audience with His Holiness, and was only kept waiting about twenty minutes before I was ushered into Larry Joe's inner sanctum. The only way he's remained chief the last two years is he's the best ass-kisser in the business, and his lips are permanently attached to the butt of Lloyd Macon, the mayor of Longbranch. One of these days, I figured, old Lloyd was gonna get voted out of office or retire, and then, if there was any justice in this world, old Larry Joe'd be out of a job.

Larry Joe was a medium-tall, real skinny guy with an Adam's apple bigger than Dallas. He was in his mid-thirties or thereabouts, divorced, and in trouble occasionally for failure to pay child support. There'd also been rumors here and there about sexual harassment at the police department. I do know Larry Joe had never hired a woman for anything more than clerical duty, and the one woman Emmett had hired as an officer had quit in a huff last year, just short of bringing charges. I heard there was a financial settlement involved.

If any of this sounds like I wasn't real fond of Larry Joe January, it's probably because I'm not.

When I walked in his office, Larry Joe neither stood up nor offered his hand for a shake. He's that kind of asshole. I said, "Larry Joe, how you doing?"

He said, "What do you want?"

"Thought maybe you and me could have a little discussion."

"About what?" he asked. He wasn't looking at me but down

161

at his desk, which was pretty much clean. I doubted Lloyd Macon let Larry Joe do much paperwork. I wasn't sure the boy could read.

"Seems like we got us a little problem. Larry Joe, you wanna look at me when I'm talking to you?"

He jerked his head up and narrowed his eyes at me. "What?" he said again. The boy was a real conversationalist.

"Looks to me like there's a little abuse of privilege going on around here," I said.

Larry Joe jumped to his feet. "I never laid a hand on her!" he screeched.

Well, he had me there. I wondered if the "her" he was referring to was the officer who quit last year in a huff, or if there was a new "her" causing old Larry Joe some problems. I thought it might be fun to find out.

"That's not exactly what she says," I said, keeping my voice even, but shaking my head in sorrow at the wrongness of it all.

Larry Joe sat back down. "This ain't nothing to do with the county," he said. "So just stay the hell out of it."

"Be that as it may," I said, which I thought was both kinda classy and as well as neutral.

Larry Joe sighed. "Look, I don't know what she told you, but it never happened, okay? She's a kid and I don't mess with kids! And if her and her mother have come to you with this, well, all's I can say is, it's the shits!"

"Her mama's upset," I said.

"And when ain't Aleeta Haines upset?"

Aha, I thought, light was beginning to dawn. "So you're taking all this out on my deputy?"

"What's that supposed to mean?" he said, his eyes narrowing even further, if that was possible.

"Your boys have been stopping Jasmine Bodine for no reason, ticketing her for things that, well, seems to me some of 'em might have done themselves. Like a broken taillight. Ask your boy Dample about it."

Larry Joe leaned back in his chair and sighed. "Jesus H. Christ on a bicycle," he said, mostly under his breath. "That woman is turning into a real nightmare."

"You didn't know about this?" I asked.

Larry Joe leaned forward and looked into my eyes. "I swear, Milt, I had nothing to do with this. Miz Haines can get carried away, you know that."

"So you diddled her little girl, huh?" I asked. I shook my head. "Larry Joe, that's real bad. You do this before or after she started turning tricks?"

Larry Joe stood up. "Get out of my office," he said, his voice mean. "I'll talk to my boys about harassing your deputy, but that's it, Kovak. I ain't talking about anything else."

I stood up. "You know we arrested Melanie for prostitution, Larry Joe. It's probably gonna come out who all she's been keeping time with for money." I smiled real sweet. "Best get that ol' résumé up-to-date," I said, and left, a grin firmly in place.

I figured Jasmine's problems were just about solved, so I decided to concentrate on Trent Marshall. The boy needed to be found and I figured that needed doing pretty damn quick. How did he get to a phone? Was someone holding him hostage? Is that who took the phone away so abruptly? Or was this all a ruse on Trent's part? Or the Marshalls'?

I'd searched the Seven Trumpets top to bottom. Unless he was being held in one of the trailers, I had to admit that maybe Brother Grigsby and his flock weren't involved in Trent's disappearance. Which bothered me a lot. I truly wanted to hang something on that bunch.

Bobbie,

That's what I'm saying! Somebody's got to do something! Clifford and I have gone to Taylor and met that Naomi Woman, but none of them will have anything to do with us because we're both underage! Trent and Amanda were both eighteen. That's the key! What do you think?

Marlene

Marlene,

I found Naomi Woman's e-mail address and I e-mailed her. Would you believe she's very interested in me? Ha-ha! Wants me to come to a meeting they're having tomorrow. Big talk about Grigsby. I've been very interested. Think I'll get an invite to the retreat!

Bobbie

Leonard,

I think I've started something maybe I shouldn't have. I'm getting scared. I wanted to help Uncle Milt find out who killed that girl Amanda, and I thought that Clifford and I could go into the retreat undercover, but they found out how old we are

164

and won't have anything to do with us. Anyway, I told Bobbie—
you remember her, right?—about this and she's decided she's
going to go undercover! Leonard, I'm scared. What if something
happens to her? It will all be my fault! I couldn't live with
myself. Help!
 Marlene

Marlene,
 Jesus, what have you done now? I can't leave you alone for a
minute, can I? Give me Bobbie's e-mail address and I'll put a stop
to this crap right now!
 Leonard

Leonard,
 It was a good idea! I just don't want anyone else hurt. God,
you can be a pain sometimes. Her e-mail address is
lawsweetie@edu.ok. Just don't be an idiot with her, okay?
 Marlene

Lawsweetie,
 Can't say that's the most adult screen name I've witnessed, but
what can you expect? Look, Marlene e-mailed me about your
stupid plan, which is just that! Stupid! Don't get involved in this—
leave it to my Uncle Milt. He's a professional. Marlene is a
child, in case you haven't noticed, so taking her advice on
anything makes you even more childish! So call this off now!
 Leonard

Leonard,
 I won't lower myself to comment on your comment about my
screen name, but what can one expect from someone named
Leonard, for Christ's sake? As for any plans I may have, they
are definitely none of your business. I assume Marlene talked to

you because she's your baby sister and thinks highly of you for no other reason than you were born before her. I've been a great help to the sheriff in the past and see no reason to end my collaboration with him. But again, none of this is your business, so kindly bug off!

Lawsweetie and proud of it!

Marlene,

I can't believe you e-mailed your brother! What were you thinking? I know he's your brother and you want to think highly of him, but as far as I'm concerned Mr. Leonard Hotshot Hotchkiss is a misogynistic stick in the mud and I could care less what he has to say! Please keep him out of this! If you want me to keep you informed on what I'm doing, I'll be glad to, but as long as you promise to keep Mr. Thinks-he's-hot-stuff out of it!

Bobbie

Bobbie,

I'm really sorry I said anything to Leonard. I know he can be straitlaced sometimes, but he is my brother and I've relied on his thoughts and feelings for a long time. Maybe too long a time. This is real grown-up stuff we're doing here, and it scared me. Clifford is no help WHATSOEVER! He thinks the whole thing is silly—which means he's scared shitless! Just tell me what you want me to do and I'll do it. It may just be the two of us, but WE ARE WOMEN AND WE ARE STRONG! Right?

Marlene

Marlene,

You are SO right, sister! I'm going to find out what happened to those kids up there! That Brother Grigsby is an asshole and he's definitely at the bottom of whatever is going on, I met with Naomi Woman and I've been invited to go to the retreat this weekend. Do you have a cell phone? I can borrow my mother's to take with me. She's always screaming about me taking her cell phone whenever I go on the road, and she thinks I'm going to Tulsa to stay with my friend Sherry. (Don't worry, Sherry thinks I'm having a fling with a guy and she'll cover for me.) If you have access to a cell phone, give me the number and keep it with you over the weekend—be sure it's charged!—and we'll keep in contact that way. Mom's cell is one of those tiny flip things and I can hide it in my underpants if I have to. I'm not sure if they're going to search me or not. My first time as a cult groupie, you know. Ha-ha! E-mail me with the number. Mom's is 555-4224. Try not to call it 'cause we don't want them hearing it ring, right?

Bobbie, your sister-in-crime!

Leonard,
Bobbie's going in this weekend! I'm terrified! What have I done? What if something happens to her? What am I going to do?

Marlene

Marlene,
When is she going? Is she going to Taylor and riding with that group there, or is she going from her place?

Leonard

Leonard,
She's going from her place. On Friday afternoon. Why?

Marlene

Marlene,
What's her address? Don't tell her I'm coming, but she's not going in there alone!

Leonard

167

Leonard,

She lives on Strand, behind the Methodist Church. Leonard, be careful! If anything happens to you, I'll die!

Marlene

Marlene,

Cool it. Everything's going to be okay. What kind of car does she drive? And what time is she leaving? Find out for me but don't tell her, you dope! Whatever you do! Got me?

Leonard

Leonard,

Don't call me a dope! Yeah, I've got you. She drives a Toyota Celica, metallic blue, and she's leaving at noon on Friday. BE CAREFUL!!!!!!!

Marlene

12

Friday dawned wet and nasty again. We were having a wetter than usual spring, but the aquifers could use the water and my wife's garden surely could. Personally, I love a good rainstorm, with lightning and thunder, the whole works. Except for tornadoes. Lord, I don't like tornadoes. When you live in tornado alley as I do, even if you love a good rainstorm, you keep one eye on the sky for funnel clouds at all times. It's just the way we live in this part of the country. Everybody who can has a storm cellar, and people living in trailers start praying with the first raindrop. But this day, this Friday, it was just rain. No lighting, no thunder, and, hopefully, no tornadoes.

I took Johnny Mac to day care, my last trip this week. They were doing a special song that day and he wanted me to stay and listen, which I did. I know it may sound silly to say it, but my kid's got a real good voice and he remembers all the words to most songs. He's a genius.

Jasmine was just leaving as I got to the shop.

"Hey, Milt," she said, a big smile on her face.

"What's up?" I said, surprised to see her smiling. She didn't do that too often on a good day, and things hadn't been going all that well for her.

"Troy came by my place yesterday," Jasmine said, Troy being one of the city police officers, the one who hadn't given her a ticket. "He said the chief jumped all over Andy about my taillight! Put him on desk duty for a week!" Jasmine laughed. A rare and beautiful privilege. Then she blushed. "He asked me out," she said quietly.

"Andy?" I asked, confused.

Jasmine rolled her eyes. "No, dummy, Troy!"

"Oh," I said, and smiled. Jasmine had been divorced for about three years. It should have been a lot longer, since everybody in town knew Bubba Bodine had been messing around on her with anything he could get his hands on from day one. The whole thing had come to a head, so to speak, when Jasmine actually caught him in her bed with another woman. She chased the woman off, cuffed Bubba to the bed, and commenced to circumcise him. Without the use of anesthesia. I talked Bubba into not pressing charges, though it was touch-and-go there for a while.

Jasmine and Emmett had had a brief flirtation a couple of years ago, shortly after his wife died, but Emmett just didn't have the heart to carry through on it. I think Jasmine had been disappointed, and I knew she hadn't dated much since the divorce. So Troy was indeed a blessing. Anything that could make this lady smile was a blessing.

"You gonna go?" I asked.

She smiled. "Maybe," she said, and headed for her car, which I noticed had a new taillight. I wondered if Troy had had anything to do with that.

I went into the shop, happy for Jasmine, almost forgetting I still had a murderer on the loose, whether he was Trent Marshall or not. And if he wasn't Trent Marshall, then I had

170

a missing kid who could be in a great deal of danger. That thought sobered me up and I called Emmett into my office. I needed a sounding board, and Emmett was pretty good at that.

"Jasmine okay?" he asked.

"Yeah," I said. "Old Larry Joe actually did something about the harassment. Chained old Andy to a desk. And looks like Troy asked Jasmine out on a date."

Emmett nodded, somewhat sadly. "Yeah, the girl needs a social life," he said.

And I wondered for the first time in a long while if maybe Emmett regretted not continuing what he'd started with Jasmine. That girl wasn't the only one who needed a social life. Other than coming out to my house on occasion to watch a ball game, I didn't know if Emmett did anything else to get out of the house.

I decided to leave that problem for another day, and concentrate on the problem of the murder of Amanda Nederwald. No matter how you looked at it, the girl was still dead and somebody killed her.

I'd already told Emmett about the telephone call from Trent Marshall to his folks, so we discussed it a bit.

"He kilt the girl, Milt. No doubt in my mind," Emmett said.

"Then why did he call his folks? And why did he ask after Amanda?"

"Throwing us off his track, more 'n likely," Emmett said. "He's hiding out, realizes what he's done and how bad it's gonna be for him; now he's trying to cover his tracks. Remember what stock he comes from, Milt."

Emmett wasn't referring to Trent's mother, my ex-lover, because he didn't know about that. He was referring to Trent's natural father, Jerry Johnson, now on death row. I guess Emmett was thinking, "Like father like son," but I couldn't help thinking that maybe he was wrong.

171

"You know, I talked to Jean about that once," I said, hoping the learned opinions of my psychiatrist wife would carry some weight with Emmett, "and she said heredity had little to do with criminal behavior—"

"Yeah, but it does have something to do with violence. And heredity isn't the only thing here, Milt. The boy knows what his father's done. Don't you think that affects him? Messes up a kid? 'My daddy killed women. Does that mean I'm gonna kill women, too? Oops, I killed my girlfriend. She's a woman. Guess I'm just like my daddy.'"

I smiled. "Jean would call that oversimplification."

Emmett grinned back at me. "Bet she says that to you a lot, huh?"

I leaned forward in my chair. "All I'm saying is, I'm not so sure this kid hurt the girl, Emmett. My money's on Grigsby. That guy's no good and we both know it."

Emmett shook his head. "No history of violent behavior."

"Yeah, well, maybe we should check and see what *his* daddy did," I shot back.

"We searched the retreat, Milt. The buildings and the grounds. The kid ain't there."

"I know, I know," I said, getting exasperated. "I just don't know where else to look, to tell you the truth."

"Maybe we should search his parent's house," Emmett said.

"Say what?"

"How do we know there really was a phone call? How do we know the kid didn't come home the next day and the parents have been hiding him out there ever since?"

"'Cause they got two other kids in that house, and one thing I know about kids, having lived with Jewel's three, you don't get to keep secrets."

"So have they got a weekend place somewhere? These people are rich, right? Maybe they got a lake cabin or something."

"Why would they hide the boy and then call me to find him?" I demanded.

" 'Cause the mama called you *before* the girl got killed, right, Milt? By the time we know the girl's dead, she'd gotten the ball rolling and couldn't stop it. Meanwhile, her kid comes to her, confesses he didn't *mean* to hurt the girl, and Mama hides him. With or without stepdaddy's knowledge."

I didn't like it, but it made sense. Emmett didn't know it, but he was hitting on something that had a right ring to it. Laura would do just what he said. Whether the kid killed her accidentally or not, Laura would cover for him. Hide him. Try to make it all go away. She had a history of doing that kind of thing, and only I knew it.

And he was right about another thing: the chances were good that the Marshalls had another home. When I'd first met Laura, she'd lived in the house I lived in now, out in the country, and she and the kids had horses. The Marshall home I'd been in had been a city house; I could see Laura having a country hideaway somewhere.

But how could I find out? Call Dixon Marshall and ask him? And if he was involved, the kid would be long gone by the time I got there. Even if he wasn't involved, he'd say something to Laura, and Laura would make sure her son was nowhere to be found.

But the county records in Tejas County could tell me if Dixon Marshall owned another dwelling. Or Laura, for that matter.

"Call Bill Williams," I said to Emmett. "See if the county records show another domicile for either Dixon or Laura Marshall."

Emmett stood up. "Sounds like a good idea," he said, leaving my office. He didn't say "I told you so," but he would if the kid was being hidden by his parents.

I went to the Longbranch Inn for lunch and found Roy Higgins sitting by himself behind a heaping plate of beef ribs, potato salad and pinto beans.

I pulled up a chair and he said, "They got key-lime today."

"Damn," I said. "Loretta," I called to the waitress, "I'll have what he's having. And two key-limes at the end, okay?"

"Milt, one of these days I'm gonna call Jean and tell her exactly what you eat here every day," Loretta said.

"And take a chance of losing your best customer? I think not," I said, grinning at her.

"At least have something green with it," she insisted. "How 'bout a side a slaw for both of you?"

We nodded and she moved to the kitchen to place my order.

"What's up with the Seven Trumpets?" Roy asked.

I shook my head. "Nothing new. Though I do want to thank you for the time Bobbie put in for me. She's real good on the computer."

"The girl's a whiz," Roy agreed, getting barbecue sauce all over his face from the rib he was gnawing on. "I even let her have a half-day off today," he said. "She's going out of town. Gotta let the girl have some vacation sometime, though I might have to close shop. Not sure I know how to answer a phone," he said and grinned.

"What with all that extra education," I said, "seems you woulda picked that up somewhere."

"But if I answer the phone, Milt, I might have to talk to a client. Then I'd have to charge them. That means I'd have to write down times and what not or Bobbie'd get p.o.'d at me. That's a lot of work."

I shook my head. "Roy, you are one lazy son of a bitch," I said.

174

"Not lazy, my man. I'm a conservationist. I just conserve personal energy, that's all."

"Hear anything from our mutual buddy, Truman Conchfeld?" I asked.

Roy shook his head in disgust. "He left for Tulsa, but then he came back. Seems little Yvette called up crying her eyes out, so he came home. She wants to move in with him. Promises to be good."

"Doesn't he live with his brother? What was his name, Sherman?"

"Yeah, Sherman called me. Asked if he killed Yvette would it be justifiable homicide. I told him I doubted it, but suggested if he hid the body nobody'd probably go looking for her."

I gave Roy a look. "Okay, I didn't say that, but I thought it," he said. "But I gotta tell you, that client you got me is dumber than dirt. Taking back that girl!"

"What can I say, Roy? The boy's in love."

Roy shook his head. "And love does make dopes of us all, don't it?" he said.

I thought about my love life over the last fifty-some-odd years. And yeah, he certainly had a point.

I was on my way home that Friday evening when I got a call from Gladys. I hadn't been fast enough to get out of range.

"Milt?"

"Yeah, Gladys?"

"Those boys at the Baghdad Apartments?"

"Yeah?" I asked, my heart sinking. "The Conchfeld brothers?"

"Yeah, that's them. Got a report of shots fired."

"Shit," I said, under my breath, I thought, but Gladys said, "No cussing on the radio, Sheriff."

"Out," I said and hung up, turning my Cherokee around and putting the little bubble light the county had finally coughed up the money for on the roof. I headed for the Baghdad Apartments.

The Long Branch Memorial Hospital didn't have an ambulance; instead, whenever one was needed, the Johnson Brothers Funeral Home's hearse was put into service. Gladys had called them and we both arrived at about the same time.

I saw the blood as soon as I hit the stairs to the second-floor apartment. The door had yet to be fixed and still hung loose, a bloody handprint smeared across it. As I got nearer I could see a body. He was sitting up, his eyes open, and he looked at me. Lord Almighty, I thought, he's not dead.

Another shot rang out and I hit the deck, grabbing my service revolver as I did. Buddy Jacobs, the hearse driver, hit the deck behind me, saying, "Oh, shit, we're all gonna die!"

"Shut up," I said.

"Sherman," I whispered to the boy leaning against the broken door. He was holding his arm, blood dripping between his fingers from a wound to his shoulder. "You okay?"

"Not really," he said quietly. "I think I've been shot."

"I can see that," I whispered. "Who's doing the shooting?"

"Who do you think?" he asked disgustedly. "Yvette."

Another shot rang out and Sherman hunkered down.

"Where is she?" I asked.

He nodded toward the rest of the apartment. "Right there," he said.

I belly-crawled forward a couple of paces to see into the apartment. Yvette was standing in the middle of the living room, holding a very large gun with two hands, pointing it this way and that, obviously in deep concentration, one eye closed as she attempted to aim.

"Who's she trying to shoot?" I asked Sherman.

176

"Me," he said, his voice resigned.

I grabbed his bad arm, as it was the closest to me, and began dragging him out of the doorway. Sherman screamed from the pain and another shot rang out, this one hitting the door just inches from Sherman's head.

"Anybody else in there?" I asked as I got him out of the line of fire.

"Truman's in there somewhere," Sherman said.

"He been hit?" I asked.

Sherman tried to shrug, then thought better of it. "Don't know," he said.

I looked behind me. Buddy Jacobs still hugged the floor of the second story. "Buddy, get him to the hospital," I said.

Buddy nodded and inched his way toward Sherman. "Can you walk, man?" he asked.

Sherman rolled his eyes. "I got shot in the arm, asshole."

"Right," Buddy said, and led Sherman down the stairs.

I inched closer to the doorway. When another shot rang out, I sank back out of sight. Surely the girl would run out of ammunition eventually, I thought. Then I remembered poor Truman was still in the apartment.

"Yvette!" I called out. "It's me, Sheriff Kovak. Remember? I helped you before when you had trouble with Truman. Remember?"

"*Sí*, I remember. I keel you too!" Another shot rang out.

I tried counting but I wasn't sure how many she'd fired before I got there, or even what caliber the gun was and how many shots it held.

"Now why you wanna kill me, Yvette?" I asked. "I helped you, remember?"

"You take away my Truman!" she said, rolling the *r* for all she was worth. "You want us to be apart! I keel you all!"

"Honey," I heard, a plaintiff sound from somewhere deeper

inside the apartment. "You don't wanna go shooting the sheriff, sweetie. You need to put the gun down, darlin', so we can talk."

"You sweetie this, darlin' that, don't give me that shit!" she screamed, the Latino accent gone. "You all hate me!"

"Yvette, you know that's not true," Truman pleaded. "You know I love you."

"Then why did you leave me?" she wailed.

"But I came back!" Truman insisted.

His voice was getting closer. I looked around the corner of the doorjamb and saw him coming out of the kitchen, hunkered down, his face pleading.

"Darlin', you know I love you. I couldn't stay away. See? Here I am, back with you. Put the gun down, honey."

Yvette turned to face him, lifting the gun again with both hands, pointing it at Truman's chest. I got up on one knee and sprinted off, flying into the room and tackling the little eighty-pound felon all by myself, visions of my high school football days in my head. Yvette went down and the gun flew out of her hands, landing at Truman's feet.

Truman picked the gun up and looked at it, then at Yvette, still on the floor from my tackle. I was kneeling on the floor, looking up at him. "Give me the gun, son," I said.

"She killed my brother," Truman said, lifting the gun to point it.

"Sherman's okay, Truman. I swear to God. He got shot in the shoulder, that's all. He's on his way to the hospital now. You need to put the gun down and go see your brother, Truman."

Yvette was still on the floor, sobbing for all she was worth. Luckily she didn't say anything. I'm afraid if she'd actually opened her mouth, Truman might have shot her. Instead, he let the gun drop to the floor. I got up and picked it up and went to the phone on the coffee table, calling for backup.

I was late getting home, which seemed to have put my wife in a randy mood. Johnny Mac was down for the count, and Jean had fixed a candlelit dinner.

"It's Friday night, Milt," she said. "Let's celebrate."

You know, it's the little things, especially when you're a parent. A Friday night and the kid's asleep, a shared look when he does something really special—funny or smart or silly—standing together and watching him sleep, peaceful at last, looking like an angel instead of acting like a devil. The little things. Life is full of them, and this was one of those Friday nights. I pushed thoughts of Truman and Sherman Conchfeld out of my mind. Completely forgot about gun-wielding Yvette. And never gave a thought to Trent Marshall, Amanda Nederwald, or the Seven Trumpets.

Maybe I should have.

13

Saturday morning, around 10 A.M., while I was upstairs in the playroom explaining to my son how you shouldn't try to put toy trucks up the cat's butt, the phone rang. Jean grabbed it downstairs, then hollered up to me that Emmett was on the line.

I picked up the extension in the playroom.

"Hey, Emmett, what's up?" I asked.

"Got a call from Bill Williams late last night. Got the info on the Marshalls' country place. They got one, all right."

"Yeah, well, go figure. Where is it?"

"In Tejas County, about thirty minutes from their city place. It's a ranch with horses and a couple living on the grounds."

"So if the kid's there, somebody knows it."

"You'd think," he said. "Think we need a warrant?"

"Yeah. Call Judge Rodgers, see if you can get one for today. Then call me."

"You love this delegating stuff, don't you, Milt?"

I grinned. "It ain't half bad," I said and hung up.

Thirty minutes later he called back. "Got the warrant."

"That was fast," I said.

"Judge Rodgers was eating breakfast, wanted to get rid of me."

"Huh," I said. "Have to talk to him more often during mealtimes."

"Seems like a workable plan," Emmett said.

"Meet you at the shop in twenty," I said, hanging up.

Then I went downstairs and explained to my wife why I wasn't going to be able to clean the gutters this Saturday either.

The Marshalls' country place was just as described: thirty minutes outside of Lydecker, about a hundred acres of trees and fields, with several horses running. White rail fences and a horseshoe-shaped gate with a brand for a name.

The gate was closed but there was a buzzer by it and we pushed it. A tinny speaker emitted sounds. We finally worked out that somebody wanted to know who we were and what we wanted.

Since this was Tejas County and not Prophesy County, Emmett and I had gone by Bill Williams's house and picked him up for the ride. He was a little skeptical of the warrant, seeing as how it was a Prophesy County judge who'd signed it, but a quick call to one of Tejas County's judges confirmed for Bill that we could serve our warrant in his county.

Bill was driving a Tejas County Sheriff's Department car, so he was the one who spoke to the voice on the other end of the tinny intercom.

"This is Sheriff Williams. We got a warrant to search the house and grounds," he said.

The tinny voice came back, "Is Mr. Marshall aware of this?"

"Don't know," Bill said. "Don't matter. Let me in now or you'll be in violation of the law."

There was a brief silence, then the tinny voice said, "Just a minute."

We waited for about three minutes before an old Jeep Wrangler came to an abrupt halt in front of the gate. I was beginning to think, what with the Seven Trumpets and all, I was spending way too much time waiting at gates. But then, we all have our crosses to bear.

The man who got out of the Wrangler was about seventy or thereabouts, tall and skinny with a tiny belly hanging over what looked like a rodeo winner's belt buckle. He wore a Stetson that rested on Dumbo ears, and had a red, veined nose that spoke of heavy drinking. His Levi's were threadbare and his Western-style shirt looked much-washed, a milky white that looked like it had once been blue. The boots he wore must've cost a pretty penny—a very long time ago.

"You the sheriff?" he asked as Bill got out of the car.

"Yes, sir," Bill said, extending a hand for shaking. "And you are?"

The old man looked at the hand and said, "I mostly don't shake hands with the law," he said. "Tiny Arnold's the name."

Well, I was right about one thing. That was a rodeo-winning belt buckle holding up the tiny belly. Probably one of many. Tiny Arnold had been Oklahoma's great hope for the National Rodeo Championship back in the early fifties. He'd been a hero throughout the state. I didn't much keep up with rodeo, being a football kind of guy myself, but even I'd heard of him. My mother thought he hung the moon. "Good-looking son of a gun," she used to say, and shake her head.

Then there'd been that bar fight. Tiny had won, but it had cost him. The boy he'd been fighting fell and hit his head against something, no one ever knew what for sure, but Tiny was arrested and charged with manslaughter, and ended up serving seven years in prison, not one of 'em for good behavior.

He never did win the National Rodeo Championship. Which might be why he mostly didn't shake hands with the law.

Bill handed him the warrant. "This says we can search the house and grounds," he said.

"Don't see like I used to," Tiny Arnold said, squinting at the warrant. "Since I can't rightly read this, guess we're gonna have to wait till Mr. Marshall gets here."

"No, sir," Bill said, "it don't work that way. I'll be glad to read you the warrant, but it's served and now we go in."

Tiny Arnold glared at him, then opened the gate, handing the warrant back to Bill. "Don't rightly wanna hang around having you read me no bedtime story, Sheriff. Thanks just the same."

He wrapped his long legs back into the Wrangler, turned it around smartly, and kicked up dust and rocks going back up the driveway.

"Plumb forgot that ol' felon still lived around here," Bill said.

"Was that who I think it was?" Emmett said.

"Tiny Arnold," I said. "Oklahoma's best all-round cowboy five years running."

"Beat a man to death in Tulsa," Bill said.

We got back into the car and headed up to the house.

This was obviously Dixon Marshall's taste. The gewgaws at the city house didn't follow through out here in the country. It was oak and pine and nubby fabrics, a lot of leather, and trophy heads on the walls.

And no sign of Trent Marshall.

There was a bedroom that was obviously his, boy stuff everywhere, but most of it for a boy a lot younger than Trent. I got the feeling Trent hadn't been in this room for a while,

183

and even if he had been, it wasn't because he wanted to be.

We checked the grounds, even getting into Tiny Arnold's small house. We met his wife, a Mexican woman who didn't speak much, but stuck to the kitchen where the smells were heavenly. Somehow, though, I didn't think we'd be offered any of the grub to be had.

All and all, no sign of Trent Marshall.

When we headed out the gate, though, we did meet his stepdaddy, sitting there in a big Cadillac blocking the drive.

He got out and leaned against the hood of the car, while the three of us crawled out of the squad car.

"Just what the hell do you think you're doing, Sheriff?" he asked, looking at me.

There were two sheriffs standing in front of him, but since he was looking at me, I answered. "Have to cover everything, Mr. Marshall," I said.

"You accusing me and my wife of hiding Trent?" he asked, arms crossed over his chest, a frown on his face.

"No, sir. Like I said, just covering all the bases."

"We've been cooperating with you, Sheriff," he said. "We thought we were both on the same side. Now it looks like my faith in you was ill-placed."

"We didn't see any sign of Trent on your property here, Mr. Marshall. So that's all there is to that. You want me to be thorough, don't you?"

"I don't want you accusing me and my wife of anything, Sheriff. I don't want that even a little bit."

Bill and Emmett got back into the car, while I stood there facing an angry daddy. Seemed like I did that a lot. "Mr. Marshall, you and I both know that if Laura knew where Trent was, she'd hide him in a New York minute. On the off chance she did, know where he is, I mean, it was worth our while to check this place out."

Dixon Marshall looked down at his feet. "You have a point, Sheriff. But I would have preferred you called me first, before just showing up here."

"And if your wife did know he was out here?" I said.

Marshall sighed, turned, and got back into the Cadillac. Rolling down the window, he said, "Please keep me posted, Sheriff."

"As always, Mr. Marshall," I said, and headed back to the squad car.

We went back to Bill's place. We thanked him for his help and and Emmett and I and got back in my Jeep, heading back to Prophesy County. When we were in range, my cell phone rang. I picked it up and said, "Kovak."

"Milt, John and I are at Jewel's. You need to come here right away," my wife said.

"What's up?" I asked.

"I don't want to talk about it on the phone. How quickly can you get here?"

"I have to drop Emmett back at the shop, then I'll come straight there. About twenty minutes," I said.

"Hurry," she said.

"Is everybody okay?" I asked.

"Yes. Hurry." She hung up and I looked at Emmett.

"I think I'll use the bubble light," I said.

"Gotta break it in," he agreed.

I made it to the shop in record time, dropped off Emmett at his car and headed to Bishop, where my sister and her husband lived. I cut the twenty minutes down to fifteen as I pulled in the circular drive in front of my sister's Tara-look-alike.

Everybody was in the living room—Jean and Johnny Mac, Jewel and Harmon, Carl and Marlene. And nobody looked

185

good. Marlene had obviously been crying, and even Carl looked a little red around the eyes. Jewel was in a dither and Harmon was wringing his hands. My Jean, however, being the professional she is, was in control, trying to keep everyone calm.

"What's going on?" I asked as I stepped in the door.

"Oh, God, Milt! This is all your fault!" Jewel said.

"You wanna tell me what I did?" I asked.

"It's my fault, Mama," Marlene wailed, the tears flowing freely. "All my fault!"

"You sure helped!" her mother said.

"Jewel," Jean said, "you need to calm down. Sit here. Carl, get your mother some tea."

Jewel didn't sit. Instead she turned to Jean and said, "I don't want any tea! I want my son!"

"What's going on?" I asked again.

"Leonard has been kidnapped!" Jewel said, falling onto the sofa, hands to her face.

"Mama!" Marlene wailed.

"Jeez, Mom," Carl said.

"Now, honey," Harmon tried.

"This is all your fault!" she said to me through her sobs.

"Marlene had a plan," Jean said, spitting the words out. "She thought she could help you by going undercover up at the Seven Trumpets—"

I turned and stared at my niece. "You what!?!"

"But the group in Taylor, that Naomi Woman's group, wouldn't take her and Clifford because they were underage—"

"You got Clifford involved in this?" I yelled at my niece.

"So she told Bobbie her plan and Bobbie put it into fruition. She left yesterday afternoon. To go to the retreat. She was supposed to call Marlene on her cell phone but Marlene hasn't heard from her—"

"Jesus Christ, Marlene, what were you thinking?" I yelled. The poor girl was curled up in a ball in an overstuffed chair, her face hidden in her arms.

"And meanwhile, Marlene told Leonard what Bobbie planned to do, so Leonard followed Bobbie, and now we don't know where Leonard is. He may be in the compound with Bobbie. We just don't know."

I sighed a deep sigh. "And that's it?" I asked.

"It's enough, isn't it?" my wife said.

"Oh, it's more than enough." I turned and looked at my niece. Walking over to the chair, I knelt in front of it, lifting her face to look at me. "Honey, what were you thinking?"

Marlene gulped a few times, then said, "I was trying to help, Uncle Milt. I thought . . . I thought . . . I don't know, just maybe if somebody went in undercover—I don't know," she drifted off.

"You weren't thinking, obviously," Jewel said. "And you!" she said, pointing at me. "What business did you have telling Marlene any of this to begin with? She's a child, for Christ's sake! She shouldn't even be hearing about such filth! And not only do you bring it home, you wallow in it! Telling her details!"

All eyes turned to me, including my wife's. I couldn't help realizing Jewel was right. I'd used Marlene as a sounding board, had even entertained thoughts of her going to the Academy, becoming one of my deputies. But she was just a kid. Seventeen years old. I'd had no right involving her in any case, much less one that involved kids practically her own age being killed.

"I'm sorry," I said. "You're right."

Jewel sighed and sat back down in her chair. "We can deal with that once Leonard and Bobbie are safe," she said, sounding reasonable for the first time. Knowing there was someone to blame, and that person readily taking the blame, seemed to help my sister calm down some.

I grabbed her phone and tried Emmett at home—he was already there. "Get everybody," I said, "Dalton and Jasmine, you and me. We're on our way to the Seven Trumpets."

"What's up?" Emmett asked.

"My nephew's stuck up there," I said and hung up.

I know men don't do guilt the way women do, but I felt pretty damn feminine as we headed in force up to the Seven Trumpets. This was all my fault. Every bit of it. Getting Marlene involved—getting Bobbie involved. If anything happened to Bobbie it would all be my fault. I couldn't think about Leonard. He was my own blood, and the thought that I'd done something so stupid that could end up hurting that boy made my flesh crawl.

I'd already given orders that we weren't waiting for anyone to open the gate. We'd use the department's pickup truck, which was pretty old and beat-up anyway, to ram through the fence on one side of the gate, and the rest of the vehicles would follow. I didn't want to let them know I was coming. Surprise might be the only ammunition I had.

As we rounded the bend where we could see the gate to the Seven Trumpets, I could also see a derelict Mazda parked near the gate. We slowed to see what that was about, and the door to the driver's side opened and Leonard jumped out.

I slammed on the brakes to my Jeep and the rest of the caravan followed suit. I jumped out of the car and grabbed him in a bear hug.

"Thank God you're alive!" I said.

Leonard pushed me away. "Yeah, Unc, I'm fine. But Bobbie's in there," he said.

I let him go and looked toward the compound. "You sure?"

"Yes! I followed her from her apartment yesterday, but she went in the gate with the others from Taylor before I had a chance to talk to her! I've been stuck here wondering what to do. I tried breaking in, but—"

"Jesus," I breathed, still staring at the compound.

"Want me to break the fence, Milt?" Dalton asked, eager to do his part of the plan.

I needed to rethink this. Would I be putting Bobbie in more danger if I went barreling in there? But would letting them know I was coming give them time to do something to her? Then there were the legal ramifications. Did I have the right basically to break and enter? If I had a reasonable assumption that there was a felony going on, yeah. But did I?

Sometimes it's a real bitch being in charge.

"No," I said to Dalton. "Stand down." I turned to Emmett. "Call up there, get someone to open the gate."

Emmett gave me a look, then dialed his cell phone. And we waited.

Bobbie wasn't there. The warrant was still good, so we looked. Everywhere. Bobbie wasn't there. Having been given permission to speak by Brother Grigsby, Naomi Woman told me that Bobbie had left shortly after they got there.

"Left where?"

Naomi Woman shook her head. "I don't know. She took off."

"Did she say anything to you?" I asked.

"No. I saw her walking off with a couple of our sisters who were showing her the grounds, then they said she'd decided to leave. Her stuff's gone. So what *is* your problem, Sheriff?"

I turned away from the bozo from Taylor and used my cell phone to call Roy Higgins at his home. When he answered, I asked, "You got Bobbie's home number?"

189

"Yeah, but, Milt, remember, I told you she's out of town."

Not wanting to drag Roy into this, and not having the time to explain, I said, "Just give me the number, Roy."

He gave it to me and I called it. The phone answered: "Hi, this is Bobbie. I'm busy loading my shotgun or dusting the machine gun nest, so just leave a message and if you're not another burglar, I'll call you back."

I left my cell-phone number and told her it was an emergency. Then I hung up.

Bobbie wasn't home. And if she wasn't here, where was she?

I turned back to Naomi Woman. "Which of these women told you Bobbie'd left?"

Naomi nodded toward two women cleaning dishes off the tables under the canopy. "Sister Rachael and Sister Ruth."

Ruth I knew—she was Barry's wife. I walked up to her. "Excuse me, Sister Ruth," I said, smiling like a gentleman.

She looked at me, then lowered her eyes. "Yes?" she said.

"Sister Naomi over there tells me you and Sister Rachael were the last ones with my friend Bobbie before she left. Can you tell me what happened?"

Sister Ruth and Sister Rachael, not as far along as Ruth, but still obviously pregnant, exchanged glances and then both looked down. "She decided the Seven Trumpets was not for her," Ruth said, talking to the ground.

"When did she leave?" I asked.

"This morning." She looked at Rachael. "Around ten?" she asked.

Rachael nodded and looked quickly at the ground. Then neither looked at me nor spoke to me. These were spooky people, I decided.

"So you're saying she left this morning around ten A.M.?" I reiterated.

"Yes," Ruth said, still not looking at me.

190

"Where did she go?" I asked.

"I don't know," Ruth said. Then she looked me square in the eye. "She didn't say." Her eyes went immediately to the ground.

"Are you through interrogating my people?" Brother Grigsby asked behind me.

I turned around. "Your friend obviously came here under false pretenses, Sheriff," Grigsby said. "And she left just as quickly as she came. Not as good an operative as you thought she'd be, huh, Sheriff?" Grigsby smiled and I wanted to slam my fist down his throat more than I wanted a really good chicken-fried steak.

"Grigsby, I'm taking you down," I said. "Somehow, someway, I'm taking you down."

I turned and got in my Jeep, leaving the compound before I did something really stupid.

"Oh, Jesus," Roy Higgins said, holding his gut like it hurt. "You're shitting me."

"I wish I was, Roy. I really do," I said.

I'd just told him about Bobbie.

"Her mama's gonna kill us both," Roy said. He looked at me with fear in his eyes. "I mean it, Milt. You don't know her mama. She's gonna gut us like chicken."

"You didn't have anything to do with this, Roy. I'll tell her that. But the problem right now isn't Bobbie's mother, it's Bobbie. We got to find her."

"How?" Roy demanded.

"If she left the compound, where would she go?" I asked.

Roy threw his arms up in the air. "I don't know! How would I know? Jesus, Milt, what have you done?"

I was getting it from all sides, but I deserved it. Bobbie was missing and it was all my fault.

We'd gotten Leonard and his borrowed dilapidated Mazda away from the compound. He wasn't speaking to me either. Like the rest of the world, he'd decided this whole thing was my fault. He'd gone home to his mother and I could only hope there had been a happy reunion. I didn't dare follow. For one thing, I had to find Bobbie and I had to find her fast. For another thing, I didn't feel like being pulled through barbed wire again. Which is what it feels like when you got seven or eight sets of accusing eyes bearing down on you.

So, after getting Roy mad at me too, I headed back to the shop. At least there the accusations would be quiet ones, since I was the boss.

What can be worse than having everybody you love or even like righteously mad at you? I'll tell you what: Walking into the sheriff's department and seeing my ex-wife and her new husband standing at the counter talking to Gladys—that's what.

I almost turned around and left, but Gladys spied me and said, "Well, Sheriff, lookee who's here!"

LaDonna and Dwayne Dickey turned and looked at me, Dwayne sticking out his hand to shake as if we were old buddies. "Hey, Milt, how you?" he said.

I shook his hand and said, "What brings y'all here?"

"We're having the annual Spring Fling at the country club and Dwayne and I are in charge," LaDonna said with pride. It had always been a bone of contention between us that, even if I could've afforded it, I would never have joined the country club. Not my style. "We need to talk to you about getting some off-duty deputies for traffic control."

"Gladys can help you with that. Just check and see who'll be off duty during the time and see if they're interested in making some spare change. You're gonna pay them good, now aren't you, Dwayne?" I asked, smiling like I cared.

192

"Probably better than they make here," he said, and guf-
fawed.

LaDonna grinned and playfully slapped her husband on the
arm. "Now, Dwayne," she said. "Be nice!"

I smiled and headed for my office. It wasn't until I was
almost to my door that I realized Dwayne had followed me.

"Such a shame about Bert's land up there by the river," he
said, shaking his head and taking a seat by my desk, uninvited.
"Such a pretty piece of property. God, can you image? One-
acre homesites! All the amenities! It woulda been worth mil-
lions."

"Now it belongs to a church," I said, for the first time de-
lighted with the thought.

"You know, Bert and I went to high school together. We
used to take girls out there to the river." He looked over his
shoulder, then winked at me. "Now don't you go telling
LaDonna!"

I laughed like I was supposed to.

"We'd get us a couple of six-packs and a couple of girls and
hang out by the river. And if you wanted some privacy,"—
wink, wink—"there was always the caves. Bert had one fixed
up with a mattress and a gas lantern—"

Marshall: "Echo-y sounding. Like he was in a cave . . ."

I'd thought it was just an expression. Echo-y sounding, like
a cave. But maybe it had been literal and even Marshall didn't
know it.

I leaned across my desk and gave Dwayne a look. "Tell me
about the caves," I said.

193

14

It was five o'clock before I got rid of Dwayne Dickey. Too late to go to the compound tonight. I needed daylight to explore the caves.

It made me sick to think I'd walked right by that rock formation and never thought about caves. Chances were real good that those caves were where Trent Marshall was hiding—or being held captive, if he was still alive. And that maybe Bobbie was there, too. Because she sure wasn't at her apartment, and her mother, when I had Jean call her, said she was in Tulsa visiting a friend. Jean got the number and when I got Marlene, against her mother's wishes, to call the friend in Tulsa, the friend, Sherry, told Marlene the cover story she'd been told: Bobbie was having a hot weekend somewhere with a man. Leonard's name was mentioned, but I'm the only one Marlene told that to.

I had everybody galvanized to meet at the crack of dawn in the parking lot of the sheriff's department. Dalton had a cousin who was a spelunker and had all the gear for cave exploring. He'd be in the parking lot too.

I didn't sleep a wink Saturday night, and I know Jean was

also tossing and turning a lot. She got up with me Sunday morning and got Johnny Mac ready. She would drop me off at the sheriff's department and then she and Johnny Mac would spend the day worrying with everybody else at Jewel's house.

When Jean dropped me off, I spotted the beat-up Mazda among the other cars and trucks. Leonard was standing in a group with Jasmine, Emmett, Dalton, and his cousin Wayne.

I pulled Leonard aside. "Go home," I said.

"No way," he said.

"Now," I said.

He pulled away from me and headed back to the others.

"Leonard, you are not deputized. You are not going."

He headed for the Mazda. "Then I'll just follow along behind. Hope I don't get in any trouble," he said.

There had been a time in my life where I'd wished for family. Now I thought of that old curse: Be careful what you wish for, you may get it.

I sighed. "Get in the squad car," I said.

I led the procession, me in the squad car with Emmett riding shotgun and Leonard in the back, blissfully unaware that the only way he could get out of the backseat was if I let him; Jasmine and Wayne in another squad car, and Dalton pulling up the rear with the pickup truck. Now I had a legitimate reason to break down the fence and damned if I wasn't gonna do it.

We got to the Seven Trumpets and I waved Dalton forward. Rolling down the window, I said, "Break it down."

There was a grin on his face while he maneuvered the pickup for a running start, then slammed through the fence, smashing barbed wire and splintering fence posts. He rolled back and forth over the fence a few times, popping one of the tires of the pickup, then pulled the truck out of the way, letting me lead the other car through. Jasmine stopped and picked Dalton up, then we turned on our sirens and headed toward the road, and up to the compound.

People were falling all over themselves when we got there. We didn't see anybody in half-dress as you would at a normal raid like this, as they all seemed to wear the same pajamas to bed that they wore during the day, but there was some tangled hair and we saw some red and sleepy eyes.

Grigsby was the only one half-dressed. He came out of his trailer buttoning up his jeans, no shirt on his skinny, hairless chest.

"What is the meaning of this?" he yelled at me as I got out of the car. As I hadn't said anything to Emmett, he opened the back door for Leonard, much to my disappointment.

"We are again serving a search warrant on these premises, due to new information."

Grigsby ripped the warrant out of my hand. "What new information?" he demanded.

"That we missed something in our search," I said.

"What?"

I got back in the squad car, ignoring him. I started up the car and headed farther into the compound, taking the poor old Ford over dips and rocks and crevices it wasn't made for. The Ford was going to need new shocks when this was over, that was for sure.

I headed east, where there was no road, toward the rock formations. My squad car hit a big rock that tore out part of the undercarriage and we all bailed out, getting into Jasmine's Ford for the rest of the short distance.

We pulled up in front of the rock formation and got out. It looked the same as it had the last time we'd been there.

Wayne went toward the rocks and started doing something, checking this and checking that. He walked around the rocks, then hollered. We all ran to where he was. He had pulled back some shrubs and smaller rocks that covered a hole into the formation itself.

"This is it," he said. He sent Dalton back to the squad car for his equipment, donned his helmet, put a coil of rope over his shoulder, and a pick ax in his hand, and said, "See you in a few," and went inside the hole.

It was less than a minute before he called out, "Y'all get in here!"

I crawled in first, feeling the claustrophobia closing in on me but willing it away. After a short tunnel barely tall enough to crawl through on my hands and knees, it opened into a large area lit with kerosene lanterns. I saw a two-burner Coleman stove, a table with folding chairs, boxes of provisions, and several bunks. Two of them were occupied.

Leonard and I ran to Bobbie, with me untying her feet while he worked on her arms and the tape covering her mouth.

When he had her ungagged, the first thing she said was, "It's about time you showed up," looking straight at Leonard.

"You're not an easy woman to follow," Leonard said.

I could barely finish untying her feet as she was kicking, trying to get up. "You know, I've been here for almost two days. You'd think you could have reacted a little faster!"

"You're just damn lucky I got here at all! You and my sister and your stupid plan!" Leonard shot back.

"Obviously it wasn't that stupid," Bobbie said. "I happened to find him." She pointed at the other bunk.

Dalton and Jasmine were busy untying the other occupant. When he sat up, I recognized him. "Hi, Trent," I said.

He looked at me and cocked his head. "Milt Kovak, right?" he said.

"That's right."

"You're the man who sent my daddy to prison."

197

I nodded. He sighed. "Well, at least you found me." He stood up, a little wobbly on his feet.

"Son," I said, "about Amanda—"

Trent's face went dark. "I know," he said. He nodded toward Bobbie. "She told me."

"You wanna tell me what's been going on?" I asked.

"It's none of your business," a voice behind us said.

We all turned to find Sister Ruth, arms resting on her swollen belly while she pointed a great big .45 ACP at us, each in turn.

"He's mine," she said, pointing the gun at Trent. "Put him back."

"Ruth," Trent said, his voice tender, "put the gun down. You don't want to hurt anybody."

"No," she whined, "but they can't take you. I saved you. You're mine."

"That's right," Trent said. "I'm yours. All yours. But they came to get this girl here. You helped her, right? Now they can take her back. Okay, Ruth?"

Ruth looked at me. "Is that right?" she said, looking a little confused. "You'll take her but leave Trent?"

"If that's what you want," I said, having dealt with a pregnant woman not that long ago, and knowing that agreeing to anything was the best way to deal.

She lowered her weapon and sighed with relief. "I saved him, you know," she said.

"I know," I said, walking slowly up to her and taking the forty-five out of her hands.

Emmett and Jasmine moved to either side of her. "Dalton," I said, keeping my voice quiet and even, "go back to the compound and get that school bus they got there. We're gonna need more room and we only got one working vehicle."

As he went out the door, Ruth doubled over in pain. "Oh, dear Lord," she said. "It's time."

With Wayne's help, we got everybody out of the narrow opening back to the world. Dalton got there with the school bus and we loaded Ruth aboard, Jasmine and Bobbie sitting with her.

We headed back to the compound, my intention being to go straight through and out the front gate, but Grigsby was standing in the road, waving his arms, when we got near the sanctuary. Dalton, being Dalton, slowed down, then stopped. I might've run the guy down, but then sometimes I tend to blow smoke.

Dalton opened the school bus door as Grigsby jumped on the first step. "I demand to know what's going—"

Then he saw Trent. "My God—" he started again, but Sister Alma came up behind him and pushed her way on board.

She saw Sister Ruth, lying on two seats, breathing heavily, and headed toward her. "This is my job!" she said to me. "I deliver the babies!"

Ruth raised her head, saw Alma and screamed. "Don't let her near me! She'll kill me like she killed Amanda!"

Well, then all hell broke loose. Alma ran for the door of the bus that was still blocked by Grigsby, who looked as dumb as I had always figured he was. I yelled at Dalton to grab her, but Dalton, being Dalton, was a little slow and managed to grab Grigsby instead of Alma and she slipped past. I headed after her, slipping on the step of the school bus and falling on my butt, only to have Trent jump over me, followed by my nephew Leonard, with Emmett picking up the rear. Emmett helped me to my feet, and by this time I could focus enough to hear little Ruth bleating in pain.

"Emmett, get Grigsby out of the bus and hold him. Dalton, get this bus to the hospital. That girl's gonna pop any minute.

Jasmine, you and Bobbie stay with her," I yelled, then headed after the boys chasing Sister Alma. From behind me, in the school bus, I thought I heard Bobbie saying something about "women's work," but then again, maybe I just imagined it.

Alma was headed for the sanctuary, the boys right behind her. I was running, and wanted them to back off, but I didn't have the breath to yell it. By the time I got to Alma's office, off the kitchen of the sanctuary building, Alma was pointing another big ol' forty-five at my nephew and Trent.

I stopped at the doorway, taking it all in. I'd pulled my weapon at some time, and now it was pointing at her. We had us what used to be called a Mexican stand-off, before the world got all politically correct and all. I'm not sure what they call it now.

"Put the gun down, Alma," I said. "You don't wanna hurt anybody else. I'm guessing Amanda was an accident, right? Just an accident. You didn't have anything to do with Trent being kidnapped, right? We can probably get all this cleared up in a New York minute—"

"How stupid do you think I am, Sheriff?" Alma demanded, now leveling the gun at my nephew's chest. "I know a little about the law, you know. I've been in jail, and I'm not going back. You're going to have to kill me first—"

She'd been pointing the gun at Leonard, her eyes on me, ignoring Trent. I'm not sure if the boy ever played ball in high school, but he did as fine a tackle as I've ever seen. The woman went down, hitting her head on a filing cabinet, the gun flying out of her hand and landing on the desktop, and managing not to do anything silly like going off and shooting off my right ear, or anything dramatic like that. Alma was out like a light, and me and the boys just stood there for a minute, staring at her.

———

Ruth's baby was born less than an hour after we got to the hospital, and, sad to say, the little girl was the spitting image of her daddy—Barry Leventhwart. So much for my idea of Grigsby and his great plan to impregnate the world.

I was in the room with Ruth when the nurse brought the baby to her. She looked at her and then handed her back to the nurse.

"This is not my child," she said, turning her head away.

The nurse looked at me. "This is her, Ruth," I said. "Your and Barry's child."

"My child is not Barry's. My child is a product of the Light," she said. "That *thing*," she said, pointing toward the baby, "is not mine. I had a son, the son of the Light."

I looked at the nurse and indicated she take the baby back to the nursery. I pulled a chair up next to Ruth's bed and sat down. "I need you to tell me what happened, Sister Ruth," I said, keeping my voice soft and even.

"My baby must have died," she said, tears leaking out of her eyes.

"No," I said, "your baby's fine. We'll find him for you. But I need you to tell me what happened with Amanda. Remember, Ruth? Trent and Amanda. Can you tell me what happened to her?"

"They blasphemed and she had to die," she said, closing her eyes tightly. "I didn't see, I didn't see, I didn't see."

"What didn't you see, Ruth?" I asked, my face close to hers, my voice a whisper.

"I didn't see Barry with her after the Light shed his seed. I didn't see Sister Alma. No, I didn't see, I didn't see, I didn't see."

I stroked her arm, thinking I needed cooler heads than mine in on this interview. So I left the room and called Jean at

201

Jewel's house. This girl needed help, and I could think of no one better at giving it than my wife.

Before we'd left the compound, we'd found Barry Leventhwart hiding in his Airstream trailer, under the bed. He began denying any knowledge of Amanda so quickly and so vehemently that I decided we'd better bring him in. We took in Grigsby, too, just for grins, leaving a bunch of pajamaed people milling around the compound, wondering what their world was coming to.

Sister Alma was taken to the emergency room at the same hospital where they'd taken Ruth—our only hospital. We got both the men to the shop and put them in separate interrogating rooms. Since Alma was still out like a light, there wasn't much I could do but wait. Barry, however, was another story altogether.

He was a wreck. Crying, pleading, wanting to see what he referred to as "Sister Ruth's child."

"That baby's yours, Barry," I said. "One look and even Ruth knew it. You need to tell me what the scam was, Barry. I need to know right now. Telling me can help you, Barry. You don't wanna go to prison for life, do you?"

"Oh, God," he wailed, "oh, God! No, I don't wanna go to prison! It was her! All her! Alma did it! She killed the girl! I didn't have anything to do with it!"

Alma had found out early in her relationship with Theodore Grigsby that he was sterile. He didn't know it, didn't want to know. He believed, halfheartedly, in his plan to repopulate the world. He halfway believed that the world could end on the eve of the millennium, either on December 31, 1999, or on December 31, 2000. He wasn't sure which was really the end of the millennium, but he knew one of 'em had to be it.

And he knew that, with special care and diligence, he could hide his people, all his women, from whatever horror was going to happen, and repopulate the world with his seed.

That was his plan, and Alma, who'd conned more people in her life than she had a right to, believed it. But only Alma knew there was no seed to sow. She let Grigsby believe she was barren, to keep him from the knowledge that his seed would never know fertile ground. In Colorado she'd helped him gather in the young women, women who worshiped him, as Alma began to believe they should. He planted, and he planted, and he planted, but no seed grew.

When the women began to leave, she talked him into moving on, and taking the few young women left with them. They met Barry Leventhwart in Oklahoma City. He was doing so much cocaine that he'd lost his job at a big financial house and was being evicted from his apartment. He came to hear Grigsby speak, and, whether stoned or just desperate, he believed.

It was a pure and beautiful coincidence that Barry's father decided to give his children the land at that point. Barry could think of nothing better to do with his than give it to Grigsby, whom he had come to think of as his real father, the Light of his life. And in return, Grigsby had given Ruth to Barry as his wife. In name only, of course.

So the Seven Trumpets was born, and more and more people, mostly women, joined the group. But still nobody was getting pregnant. That's when Alma, according to Barry, came up with her great plan.

Brother Grigsby's seed-sowing had been a ritual in itself; there was no reason Alma couldn't improve on it. There was a room in the sanctuary they used for the "blessing," as Brother Grigsby liked to call his roll in the hay with the anointed, where each woman was brought for her "indoctrination."

Grigsby would do his thing and then leave, and Alma would take over from there.

Alma's new ritual included a cleansing cup of herbal tea before Brother Grigsby's entrance; the tea was laced with barbiturate. After Grigsby had performed and left, the women would fall asleep; that's when the real seed-sowing would happen. The "indoctrination ceremony" would be repeated as many times as necessary. Alma kept a close eye on the women of the camp and would know when menstrual periods stopped.

Barry Leventhwart was the father of every pregnant woman's soon-to-be-born in the compound.

And all had gone according to plan until Trent and Amanda appeared.

One of the few men in the compound had found Trent trying to get Amanda out. Amanda had been taken to Alma and Trent had been put in the men's tent, under guard. After Amanda's "indoctrination" by Grigsby, he left, and Barry came in. Unfortunately, Amanda wasn't totally out. Amanda was a bigger girl than most of those at the compound, and Alma's barbiturate formula must not have been strong enough; her body resisted the barbiturate, and she began to fight and scream when Barry mounted her. Trying to quiet her, according to Barry, Alma put a pillow over her face.

"I didn't know!" Barry cried. "Not until later! Then Alma told me to take her body and put it in the pasture. She told me to take Trent and—and—she wanted me to shoot him and put him with Amanda's body, but—"

"But Trent was gone when you got to the men's tent," I suggested.

Barry lowered his head and nodded, tears leaking out of his eyes and puddling on the Formica tabletop of the interrogation room.

Finally he looked up at me. "I wouldn't have done it, Milt.

204

I swear! Amanda was an accident. There's no way I'd shoot anybody."

Jean's interview with Sister Ruth told the rest of the story. Ruth had seen Barry going toward the sanctuary and followed him. She saw the whole thing and heard Alma give Barry directions to kill Trent.

She'd gone to the men's tent and found the guard asleep and Trent tied to one of the cots. She untied him and led him gratefully away, taking him to the caves to hide him.

In Ruth's mind, Trent became hers. She'd saved his life and now his life belonged to her. "I had to tie him up a little," she told Jean, smiling, "but soon he would have wanted to stay. You know how little boys are," she said, rubbing her empty belly. Tears formed in her eyes. "I was going to have a son," she said, "but he died in childbirth."

In interviewing Grigsby, we found out he didn't know squat. And I think I believed him. And he didn't believe for a minute that all that seed-sowing out at the compound had belonged to Barry and not him. Well, at least he wouldn't admit it.

We had to let him go. No charges. Nothing I could stick to him—the Teflon preacher. By the time we got up to the compound to do a follow-up, Grigsby was long gone, and there were just a few people left, mostly pregnant women, milling about without much purpose. I got county services to look into that problem.

A few days later, I had a chance to interview Trent.

"At first," Trent said, "I was glad to go with Ruth. I knew those people were going to hurt me if I stayed in that tent. But I had no idea where Amanda was," he said, his eyes filling with tears, "and I wanted to leave the cave and go find her."

We were at Trent's parents' home, the boy seated on the couch next to his mother, with me in a wingback chair across from him. Dixon Marshall sat on the other side of his stepson, his arm around his shoulders.

"Milt, he shouldn't have to talk about this!" Laura said.

"Mom, cool it," Trent said, giving his mother a look.

"He needs to talk about it, Laura," Dixon Marshall said.

Trent sighed. "When I told Ruth I needed to leave, to find Amanda, she drugged me. I guess that's what she did, anyway. She gave me something to drink and the next thing I knew I was flat on my back on the cot and my arms and legs were tied." He shuddered at the memory. "Most of the time I was alone in there, but late at night she'd sneak in and stay with me. I mean she never, you know . . ."

"Tried anything?" I ventured.

"Right," Trent said, relieved at having that out of the way. "Mostly she'd just curl up next to me on the cot and sleep. Course, she never untied me or I'd have gotten away."

"What about going to the bathroom, son?" his stepfather asked.

Trent turned red. "Well, she made me use a bedpan."

"I don't want to hear any more of this!" Laura said. She stood up. "This is disgusting! If you hadn't gotten mixed up with that cheap Amanda Nederwald—"

Trent was on his mother before either his stepdaddy or I could stop him. He slapped her in the face.

Dixon Marshall grabbed him by his arms, pulling him off Laura and I took Laura's arm. "Don't ever speak her name again!" Trent yelled at his mother. "You aren't worthy to speak her name!"

"You're just like your father!" she spat back. "No wonder I believed all along you killed her!"

I let go of Laura's arm and left the house. That kind of venom I didn't need.

———

206

All the way from Tejas County to Prophesy County I thought about what a lucky guy I was. I was on my way to Jewel's house where my whole family would be, and boy, were they pissed. But I'd never have to see or hear or think about Laura Johnson ever again. That woman was so out of my system that the mere thought of her left me a little queasy. I thought for a minute what my life could have been like if it'd taken another road all those years ago, and how, sometimes late at night, even since Jean came into my life, I'd wondered if I'd made the right decision.

Now I knew. Boy, howdy, had I made the right decision. I was a happy man, happier than I had any right to be, maybe, but happy just the same. I had Jean and Johnny Mac and my sister and her family, and some pretty damned good friends. And not one regret.

Jewel got over being mad at me. That usually happens whenever she needs something, and when Carl got his first speeding ticket, Jewel needed something. I don't confide in Marlene anymore, having learned my lesson the hard way.

Theodore Davis Grigsby was finally found back in his old stomping grounds of Baton Rouge, Louisiana. He was doing tent revivals and had a lot of young women parishioners. We still didn't have anything to charge him with, so we just told the Baton Rouge police to keep their eyes on him and let it go at that.

Alma Smith and Barry Leventhwart both pled guilty to manslaughter in the death of Amanda Nederwald. Sister Ruth, aka Cara Carlisle, was committed to a state institution by her parents; when she went away, she was still denying that the child she gave birth to was hers.

Barry was sentenced to five years in prison and asked his Aunt LaDonna and her husband Dwayne Dickey to be the guardians of his child, a little girl he named Ruth.

The last I heard, that nice piece of land on the Cullum River was still being fought over in court; my ex-brother-in-law Bert said it belonged to him, and lawyers representing Theodore Grigsby were saying different. Me, I didn't really care. As long as it stayed empty for a while, it was all right with me.

Becca Tatum and her lawyer Ass, I hear, are suing my ex-brother-in-law for liability in the death of her daughter Amanda Nederwald. It will be an interesting trial to watch, if I get the time.

"Bobbie?"

"Yes? Who's this?"

"Ah, hi, it's Leonard Hotchkiss."

There was a silence on the other end of the line. Finally, Bobbie said, "It's about time you called."

"Well, you know, I saved your life; the least you could have done is called me to say thank you!"

"Ha! As I understand it, Mr. Hotchkiss, you just basically got in the way!"

"You know, I called you to give you a chance to be a reasonable human being and thank me for what I did for you—"

"Reasonable human being? Don't you mean a dithering little female going all 'Thank you, thank you, you big strong savior, you!' " Bobbie said.

"Jesus! You are a real pain in the ass!"

Bobbie sighed. "You wanna come over?"

"You gonna fix me dinner?" Leonard asked.

"If you wanna eat, you better bring it yourself! I'm not your slave!"

"I bet you don't even know how to cook!"

"You're damned right I don't! And I'm proud of it!"

"Taco Bell?" Leonard asked.

"I prefer Burger King," Bobbie said.

"Jeez, we can't even agree on fast food!" Leonard said.

"It's a start," Bobbie said and hung up.